THE
AINSWORTH
KILLINGS OF 1879

Nebula Press: For any questions regarding usage,
please contact nebulapress@yahoo.com.
Visit the author's website at www.jlwillow.com or
contact her at jlwillowbooks@gmail.com.

First Edition.
ISBN 10: 0-9992526-7-3
ISBN 13: 978-0-9992526-7-3

Illustrations and Cover Design by Crina Magalio.
Author Photo by Krissy Rose Kleiner.
10 9 8 7 6 5 4 3 2 1

Also by J. L. Willow

A Weighted Soul and Other Dark and Twisted Tales

Missing Her

The Scavenger

To Chris:

My love, this one's for you.

N
W E
S
N
S

THE
AINSWORTH KILLINGS OF 1879

J. L. WILLOW

Prologue

Darkness crept over the farmland. A breeze whispered through the open field, dancing along the stalks of grass. Cricket song sounded from everywhere and nowhere at once. Scattered clouds hung like charcoal smears against the hazy, yellow-blue sky. The house at the top of the hill emanated an orange glow; if one peered inside, they could make out three distinct silhouettes seated at the kitchen table, presumably at supper.

But the herd held no appreciation for the blissful peace of the evening. They had spent all their lives in the open air, unprotected from the elements save for a small barn on the other side of the property. Though most of the cows had settled down inside the shelter, a few stayed out in the field. Two of the remaining creatures were a first-calf heifer named Caroline and her little one, Piper. The pregnancy had been extremely hard on Caroline and only a few weeks prior, it was uncertain whether or not she would make it. Ample rest and feed later, both mother and daughter were thriving.

Caroline always enjoyed exploring the far reaches of the field, furthest from the house and the rest of town. It was quiet there and she sometimes got a peek at wild animals in the distance, running in and out of the neighboring forest. Piper followed her wherever she went, providing Caroline a companion during her escapades. On this night, the mother quietly munched on grass and clover while her calf rested in the cool sod nearby. Caroline could tell her young one was growing weary. They would soon retire for the night. The mother mosied a few steps over to one side, chewing her cud. As she did, she raised her head to peer along the outskirts of the fence. The sun was completely hidden behind the rolling hills surrounding the farm. That, compounded with the fact that her eyesight wasn't the best, meant there wasn't much to see, so she dipped her head back down.

Without warning, the crickets ceased their song. Caroline looked up, startled at the sudden silence. Again, there was nothing she could make out, but something instinctually made her shake her head in unease. She turned toward her calf and curtly noised an order. Piper understood, standing and trotting to her mother. Caroline snorted and the two began to make their way back toward the rest of the herd in the barn.

After only a few steps, Caroline paused when a low rumbling filled the air. Piper didn't understand the source of the noise and looked left and right. The mother turned to the fence, once again staring into the night. This time, she saw a large outline blackened against the sky.

A pounding of footsteps. Caroline's hackles raised. She backed away as it barreled through the fence, sending splinters of wood flying, but she couldn't move fast enough.

It struck.

Piper shrilled as Caroline was dragged away. The calf watched her mother get pulled through the fallen barbed wire, shredding her hide and dyeing her coat maroon. The metal ripped through muscles and split sinew down to the bone. Caroline's shredded legs writhed as her hoofs pawed at the ground, but there was nothing to catch onto. She screamed, a cry of agony and for her child.

The calf stumbled forward, bleating in panic. Within seconds, the forms of the mother and the thing that had taken her dissipated into the darkness.

Caroline never stopped screaming. Piper only stopped hearing her when she was too far away for her voice to carry.

Chapter One

AUSTIN DUNKED THE brush back into the water. The suds in the bucket had been a pale gray minutes before but were now colored to a bright pink. "Levi, do I gotta keep goin'? My arms hurt."

Levi heaved a sigh and peered down at his younger brother kneeling on the ground. "Is the fence still red?"

Dropping his head, Austin glared at the stain. "Yeah."

"Then keep goin'."

As Austin grumbled under his breath, Levi dragged the back of his hand across his damp forehead. Not even an hour past daybreak and he was already sweating. It was going to be a long day, although he probably could've guessed that from the events of the previous night.

The older brother grabbed the shovel from where he leaned it against the fence and thrust it into the ground in front of him. Another clump of dirt and grass came free and he tossed it aside. The indentation of the hole was still in the soil from where the post had been pulled, but it needed to be reshaped before a new post could be staked. The splinters of wood and trails of wire resulting from the fray still littered the ground, but fixing the fence took priority over cleaning up the rest of the mess. The herd was resigned to the barn until the new fence was in place to prevent any of them from wandering off. And from their frustrated bleating, Levi could already tell they were getting irritated in the enclosed space.

When the brothers and their father heard the disturbance the previous night, they rushed out of the house without hesitation. Levi had the forethought to grab an oil lamp, but almost wished he hadn't when they came across the sight. Poor Piper was standing off to one side, crying toward the empty darkness. Caroline was nowhere to be seen and two fence posts had been unearthed. Loose wire littered the ground, splattered with scarlet. It didn't take long to piece together what occurred. Something had taken Caroline. Not just stole her, but savagely dragged her off the property. Pa had forced his face into a neutral expression and ordered Austin back inside while he investigated. Levi was tasked with herding Piper back inside the barn, along with any other cattle that had wandered out toward the noise. He had never seen a calf with such fear in its eyes. She kept crying intermittently and glancing back toward the fields as they walked. Part of Levi wanted to stay in the barn with the animal to provide some comfort in the night, but as soon as Piper was let inside, she quickly retreated into the herd.

Once the older brother returned to the house, Pa had told him to get some sleep and they would take care of the damage in the morning. But sleep never found Levi as he lay in bed, eyes open toward the ceiling. He simply couldn't erase the face of that terrified calf from his mind.

He wasn't sure he'd ever be able to.

"Levi!"

The boy glanced up. His father was just beginning to crest

the hill on the other side of the fence, approaching the house. Levi dropped the shovel in his hand and started striding toward his father. "Well," he said once he was within earshot, "didja find anythin'?"

Pa moved the clump of tobacco from one side of his mouth to the other and spit a glob onto the dirt. "Tracks led to the woods, but ended at the treeline. Seemed like she struggled quite a bit before whatever it was finally finished the job."

Levi grit his teeth. He swore he could still hear Caroline's screams echoing in his head. "Whaddya think did this?"

Pa opened his mouth to respond, but spotted Austin eavesdropping from a few yards away. He turned his back so he and Levi faced up toward the hill, away from the fence – and the prying ears. "Some sorta animal, that's for sure. Musta been pretty big and strong to get through the fence and drag her all the way back. I'm thinkin' maybe a rogue bear or somethin'."

"Do we even get bears this far out?"

The old man shrugged. "Not normally. The tracks were scuffed when Caroline struggled, so it's hard to tell. But I dunno what else coulda done it. If it killed a calf, I'd assume it was somethin' smaller like a wolf or coyote. But not many animals are strong enough to take down a full-grown cow by themselves." His expression was somber as he examined the woods in the distance. "Poor girl. I'm gonna miss her. Right after Piper was born, too."

Levi clenched his fists at his sides, his mouth sealed shut. His father was never one for expressing emotion and he especially didn't like it when his sons showed anger. He always said that the strongest men were the calmest. The ones that blew steam out of their ears always crumbled when the going got rough.

Luckily, Pa's eyes were focused on the broken fence and he didn't notice his son's internal conflict. "We gotta put some more thought into protectin' the farm. I've heard some others had their animals taken: the Wilsons' lost most of their flock to a fox a few weeks back, and the butcher on the other side of town had a hog killed, too. We've been lucky so far, but it seems like our luck has just about run out."

Levi took a breath to steady himself before replying, "What should we do?"

"Pack some stones around the bottom of the posts, add some more barbed wire…" Pa trailed off, then added, "The other thing I don't quite understand is why Caroline was killed like this. The others in town just up and vanished, no tearin' down of the fence or nothin'. What made last night different?"

His son shook his head. "I dunno, Pa."

After a few seconds of tense silence, Pa put a hand on Levi's shoulder. "You and your brother better get cleaned up and ready for school. I'll finish fixin' the fence."

"You sure? I can help when I get back."

"I oughta wrap this up within the next few hours. Otherwise, the herd's gonna end up goin' stir crazy." Pa motioned to the house and added, "Now, fetch your brother 'n get goin'. I don't want y'all to be late."

On their father's command, the boys quickly gathered up the cleaning supplies and hurried into the house. Levi ran upstairs to sweep his slate and a few pieces of chalk into a burlap sack before slinging it over one shoulder. The rustling sounds from Austin's room told him his younger brother was doing the same.

Levi paused at a mirror hanging in the hallway. His dark brown hair was plastered to his forehead and his face was coated in a thick layer of dirt and sweat. The boy ran a hand through his hair, somewhat able to flatten down the messy strands. He used the edge of his shirt to wipe the worst of the sweat and grime from his face. When he touched his fingers to his cheek, he felt the first hint of stubble bite back.

Austin passed the mirror and, upon seeing Levi, also stopped to fix his disheveled appearance. His hair was a shade darker than blonde, but more curly than straight. The boy was a head shorter than his older brother and still had a year or two to go until he really shot up in height. The most distinct feature about him was his eyes, a shade of gray-blue identical to their mother's. After her passing, Levi noticed Pa had difficulty looking Austin in the eyes for a few months. Like even just seeing the color was a painful reminder of what he had lost.

The brothers hustled downstairs, nodded farewell to their father, and headed out the door. They didn't need to think about where they were going: the footprints pressed into the dirt trail from weeks of traveling into town led the way.

Levi could feel Austin's eyes on him as they walked. It was only a matter of time before—

"What did Pa say about Caroline?"

Levi rolled his eyes, gaze fixed on the buildings slowly growing larger ahead of them. The walk to the schoolhouse wasn't long, no more than a quarter of an hour. But with Austin by his side for the entirety of it, it always seemed longer. "Nothin' important. He just said he wants to reinforce the fence, hopefully make it stronger and harder to get through."

"What does he think killed her?"

"Don't worry about it."

"Lee-vy-ee," Austin groaned, stretching out each syllable. "I'm eleven, you're only four years older than me. Stop treatin' me like a baby."

"I'm not treatin' you like a baby, Austin. You just don't need to know everythin', that's all."

His little brother huffed and crossed his arms. "You're always talkin' 'bout how I need to grow up and help around the farm more, but how am I supposed to do that when you won't even tell me what's goin' on?"

Levi picked at the dirt under his nails absentmindedly while he thought. In all honesty, Austin was right. When he was his brother's age, Pa was already telling Levi everything about the farm and how it was run, including the messy and sometimes gruesome details of owning cattle.

Then again, his mother was gone by that point. So, who else did Pa have to talk to?

"He thinks it was a bear."

Austin's head swiveled toward Levi, clearly shocked his nagging was successful. "But we don't get bears out here. Do we?"

Levi shifted, fiddling with the strap of his rucksack. "There's not much else it coulda been. No wolf or coyote is strong enough to break the posts like that, let alone drag Caroline half a mile to the woods."

Austin's eyes went wide. "The tracks led to the woods?"

"Yeah. Caroline struggled the whole way, but it looks like whatever it was eventually got the best of her."

Austin was silent for a moment. "Do you really think it was a bear?"

Levi steeled himself. "Yes."

But the true answer hung between them.

The whole day at the schoolhouse, Levi's mind wandered. It seemed like whenever he blinked, an image of blood on the fence and the torn barbed wire flashed in his mind. Pa might've been content with the answer that Caroline was killed by a lone bear, but Levi was not so easily assuaged.

While all the other students broke for lunch, Levi sat by himself toward the back of the room, absorbed in his thoughts. Eventually, he came to a decision. He would return to the scene that night. Only Pa had inspected it, after all. Maybe there was something he had missed that Levi could find. His father wouldn't approve of Levi going out to the woods, but he would be careful. Pa strongly warned against his sons getting close to the treeline, something Levi never quite understood.

Although the seconds seemed to draw out much longer than normal, they still continued to pass by until the final school bell rang at last. A few of the boys asked Levi to go fishing at the nearby creek, but the boy politely declined. He had too much on his mind. Besides, he still had work to do before the night's end.

Every person in the Oakley household had their own evening tasks: Pa fed the cattle, Austin swept the house and set the table, and Levi prepared a meal based on whatever food they had readily available. Tonight, it was roast chicken with corn mash. Levi was seated at the table, shucking the last of the corn, when a shadow skulking toward the door caught his eye.

"Where're you goin'?"

Austin attempted to subtly tuck what he was holding where Levi couldn't see. He smiled at his brother – slightly too wide. "I'm goin' to check on Piper."

Levi narrowed his eyes. "What're you holdin'?"

Defeated, Austin threw his head back and sighed, "Nothin'."

"Tell me what it is."

"Why do you care?"

"'Cause you're actin' weird."

Austin glared and revealed the item.

"A magnifyin' glass?" Levi laughed.

"Uh, yeah," Austin glared at him, offended and slightly confused. "I'm goin' back out to look at the tracks myself."

"How you gonna use that if it's dark outside?"

Austin's face fell. "Oh. Yeah, better get a lantern too."

Levi rolled his eyes and grabbed the one he was using to light the tabletop. "Was that proof enough that you shouldn't be goin' out there by yourself?"

There was a pause before Austin reluctantly nodded. "I guess," he huffed, then grimaced. "Are you gonna tell Pa?"

His older brother paused. He had been planning on going out himself regardless. And even if he told his brother not to go, it was more than likely he would sneak out of the house anyway when Levi wasn't looking. Better kill two birds with one stone: allow Austin to quell his curiosity and do some investigating of his own. "No, I won't tell," he replied slowly. "Instead… I think I'll join you."

Austin's eyes bugged wide. "Really?"

Levi shrugged. "You're right. You're gettin' older and you need to start bein' included in stuff like this. No goin' into the forest, though. Near it is fine, but no further than the treeline. You know how Pa gets about that stuff."

"Awhhh," Austin whined. "Then how am I supposed to find the bear?"

"It's probably long gone by now. Besides, our goal should not be to find it, just to identify it. If it did that to Caroline, whaddya think it could do to us?"

The boy grimaced. "Oh."

"Yeah, 'oh.' Now let's get goin' so I'm not late puttin' supper on the table. Ten minutes, tops."

"Twenty."

"Fifteen."

"Deal."

With that, the two boys strode out the front door. Levi waited until he saw his father's lantern glimmering in the barn, likely checking the herd was settled for the night, before he motioned for Austin to dim his lantern. They slowly made their way across the yard, dragging their feet slightly to avoid any missteps or sprained ankles. Normally, they would just go through the front entrance of the gate, but there was no gate along the back of the fence, so they carefully pulled back the barbed wire and stepped between the two wood rails.

Once they reached the top of the hill and the house was barely in sight, Austin cranked the lantern back up to full brightness and looked toward his brother. The thrill of anticipation fueled his smile. That and the feeling he was doing something he wasn't supposed to be doing. He pointed at their feet. "Look! There's tracks!"

Levi crouched down, running a hand along the flattened grass. "Don't really look like bear tracks. More like drag marks. Musta been what Pa was talkin' about when he said Caroline had been strugglin'." He glanced around and motioned to a spot on the ground. "Over there, that looks more like it. Could be a full print."

They moved a few feet further down the hill to a large impression in the dirt. The town was nearing its dry season, so most of the ground was pretty solid and hard to impress. Whatever made that mark must've had some weight to it. He placed his hand in the center of the print. Five large toes extended up and around his hand, nearly double the size. "Definitely not Caroline," Levi murmured.

A few moments of silence passed and Austin couldn't take the suspense any longer. "So?" he hissed. "Whaddya think?"

Levi massaged his chin with one hand, still feeling the uneven ground with the other. "From what I've seen in books, they could be bear tracks. But bears don't come this far out. There's nothin' for them to even eat out here."

Standing, Austin gestured to the left. "They seem to turn off there and keep goin'. Let's follow it!" Without waiting for his brother's reply, the boy bounded off. Levi raised his gaze to where Austin was headed.

A wall of dark, jagged trees met his gaze.

"Aus, slow down," Levi hissed, taking off after his brother. In the bouncing, golden light of the lamp, it was hard to make out details of the ground. But Levi's eyes did catch a few things while he ran.

A small tuft of white hair.

A dislodged rock.

A dark red smear.

The young boy slowed his pace as he approached the edge of the forest. Even with his giddy excitement, Austin had enough self-control to stop himself at the treeline. When Levi drew near, something about the forest made his stomach twist. Although most of the area around it appeared untouched, this section of shrubbery had bent and broken branches. The ground he could see was marred and uneven. It continued some ways into the woods, but the lantern light dissipated before the pair could make much more out.

Levi pointed to the disturbed section of brush. "That must be where the bear dragged Caroline inside."

"Whoa." Austin held the lamp further into the leaves. "I ain't never been so close before."

Suddenly, Levi felt the air shift. A wave of unease washed over him and he quickly spun around. He couldn't see much in the pale light, but the hair on the back of his neck instantly pricked up.

The air seemed to whisper, *you're not alone.*

"Austin." Levi turned to his brother. "I don't think we should be here."

"Wait." Austin leaned forward, peering around a tree. "I think I see somethin'."

Levi started to speak, but stopped when he realized – the forest was quiet, unnaturally so. No rustle of leaves, no hooting of owls. Not even the chirping of crickets.

"It looks like it's only a few steps in," said Austin, oblivious to his brother's unease. "I can reach it."

Levi grabbed Austin's arm. "I don't like it here. We gotta–"

Off to their left, a twig snapped. Levi's head twisted in the direction of the sound, his eyes wide.

He didn't feel Austin slip through his grasp.

Levi was frozen. He stared into the darkness of the trees. Even though it was pitch black, he swore he was making eye contact with something. A voice deep inside him screamed at him to run away. But it was like his shoes were nailed to the ground.

For a moment, Levi felt the whole forest hold its breath.

But then, there was a noise.

A deep, guttural growl.

Levi's heart leapt in his chest. "Austin!" Suddenly, his brother was next to him. Levi grabbed his shirt tight and started running. Sometime during the commotion, the lantern's light was snuffed, leaving only the subtle moonlight to guide them. A stray rock caught under Levi's foot and sent him sprawling across the ground. He scrambled up, refound Austin's arm with his hand, and kept running.

It was only when he crested over the hill and saw the dim

light of the house that Levi felt a flutter of relief. Once they at last made it inside the fence and came to a stop, he turned around to stare behind them with bated breath.

For the moment, it seemed like nothing had followed them.

"I… think we're safe," panted Levi. For the first time since he started running, he looked at his brother.

Austin was clutching a pelt. The gray fur draped over his two arms, glossy and pristine. Levi's gaze ran along the edge of the skin and saw that the cuts were clean. Expert, even.

Something about it made his blood run cold.

"Austin," Levi said, taking a step back. "Get that thing outta here before Pa–"

"What're you boys doin'?" The brothers both snapped their heads up to see Pa striding out of the house. Seeing him approach, Austin tried to shove the pelt behind his back, but once again, he wasn't fast enough. "What do ya have there, Aus?"

Austin looked toward Levi for support, but the older brother simply crossed his arms in disdain. The younger brother dropped his head and slowly held out his hands. As Pa grew closer, his footsteps slowed and eventually stopped a few feet away from the boy.

"Where'd you get that?" the old man snarled at the fur.

Austin took a step back, his face a mask of confusion and concern. "We were just trackin' the thing that killed Caroline."

"You went to the woods, didn't you?" Pa spat on the ground in front of the boys. "You got that thing from the woods."

"But maybe it's helpful!" Austin held the pelt up, inspecting it carefully. "It looks like a coyote. Maybe it was a coyote that killed–"

"It wasn't no damned coyote!" Pa shouted. The two brothers froze at the tone of their father's voice. A moment of silence passed and the old man closed his eyes. "Austin, drop it on the ground and go straight to your room. Levi, make supper. I'll take care of it."

Austin's face fell and Levi saw his bottom lip tremble. But his expression remained mostly neutral while he placed the blanket of fur onto the ground and headed inside. Levi followed in shortly after him. Just when he began to prepare the meat for cooking, he glanced out the kitchen window.

Pa was backlit by a small fire. His hands were in his pockets, his shoulders slouched as he stared into the flames. Levi saw the edges of the pelt curl and blacken, releasing wispy smoke into the night. As though he could sense Levi's gaze on his back, Pa looked over his shoulder.

Levi suddenly became much more interested in preparing supper.

Chapter Two

AUSTIN STAYED IN his room the remainder of the night, with the exception of a quarter hour during which he ate dinner. He kept his eyes focused on his plate as Levi and Pa made small talk about the farm and the goings on in town. Even though Pa seemed mostly over what had happened earlier that evening, Austin clearly couldn't stop beating himself up about it. His sour mood continued into the next morning as he grumbled to himself while eating breakfast. Eventually, Levi couldn't take it any longer. When they were putting on their shoes, the older brother socked the younger in the arm.

"Hey!" Austin yelped, rubbing the sore spot. "What was that for?"

"Stop with that face. Pa ain't even mad at you no more."

Austin glowered at him and continued to pull his laces taut. "I'm not makin' a face."

"Yeah, you are. Now get your head focused, we got an exam today."

The younger brother groaned before standing and tossing his bag on one shoulder. "Don't remind me."

Levi continued to lightly jest with Austin on the walk into town until eventually his mood shifted upward.

Once the brothers arrived at the one-room schoolhouse, Austin took his seat in the middle of the room and Levi moved to sit down in the chair furthest from the front of the class. As he waited for the lesson to begin, he replayed the events of the previous evening in his mind. He was hoping that taking a closer look at the tracks would help quell his suspicions, but it only left him with more questions than answers. Far too many things didn't seem right, between the weird tracks, the animal skin, and the fact it killed Caroline when Piper was standing right next to her. And the sound he'd heard last night… he'd never heard anything like it. It could've been a bear, but he didn't know what sounds a bear made, so he couldn't be certain. All he knew was he felt the presence of something else with them near the treeline. And whatever it was felt dangerous.

As he pulled a slate board from his satchel, he realized why all of this felt so wrong. The farm had always felt simple, understandable, and predictable. But this single event had thrown his whole world out of balance.

"Mornin'." Glenn sat down in his usual chair beside Levi. Although Glenn's blonde hair was normally marred with dirt, this morning it was especially dark. The boy's family owned a farm on the other side of town. While Levi's family focused on cows and chickens, Glenn's owned sheep, goats, and grew wheat. There was a level of mutuality between the families and there was never any hesitation in aiding the other if one was having a bad season. The boys grew up knowing that they could count on each other to help with anything farm-related, and that understanding soon cultivated a friendship. It was lucky that both Glenn and Levi got along so well – or unlucky, if you saw things from the teacher's perspective. They could often be found in the back of the class-room, snickering and making faces at the girls in their class.

Today, however, Glenn seemed much more subdued than usual. His normally bright eyes were dull and slightly bloodshot. He had his elbows on his desk and one hand pressed into his cheek to prop up his head.

"Mornin'," Levi greeted back before adding, "Somethin' wrong?"

Glenn dropped his gaze to his lap. "Ryder died last night."

"Awh, hell," breathed Levi, shaking his head. He had known the family dog for years. Ryder was a sweet Collie, playful, kind, and a fine herding dog. Not a bad bone in his body. "I'm sorry. What happened?"

Glenn ran a hand through his hair, jostling the already haphazard strands. It was only when he did this that Levi noticed the burgundy caked under his nails. "Some animal got him. We woke up this mornin' to the goats goin' crazy and came outside to find blood all on the ground and no sign of Ryder." He pursed his lips, glaring at nothing in particular. "My Pa thought it was a coyote or somethin', but I dunno. It left big tracks. Why didn't it go for the goats? Much easier to snatch one of them, they're nearly helpless. Why go after poor Ryder?"

Big tracks. "That's awful strange," Levi murmured, "'cause somethin' similar happened a few days ago on our farm."

Glenn turned to look at the boy in shock. "Is that right?"

"Yeah. Couple nights ago, we heard one of our calves screamin'. Somethin' took Caroline and dragged her through the barbed wire fence. Tracks led into the forest and they were bigger than any wolf or coyote I've ever seen."

His friend's eyes went wide. "Oh, poor Caroline. Right after Piper was born, too."

"Yeah, I know."

Glenn picked at the chipped corner of his slate, deep in thought. "Sounds like the same animal."

Levi shook his head. "Maybe, but the tracks didn't make sense to me. They looked like bear tracks."

"There's no bears around here."

"Exactly. But whatever it was broke through our fence. What other animal could do somethin' like that?"

Glenn frowned, saying, "I dunno. It musta been pretty strong, then."

"Pa said we're gonna start reinforcin' the fence once it's fixed, make it as safe as possible. We can't afford to lose any more of the herd."

"I'll ask my Pa if we can do the same."

The teacher entered the classroom and the chatter in the room began to quiet. Levi leaned toward his friend and whispered, "I'm not about to let this thing keep killin'. If you see or hear anythin' else about this bear, you lemme know."

"Alright, you do the same."

Maybe it was just Levi, but it felt like the rest of the day passed with a sort of haze shadowing it. Every conversation seemed forced, every lesson dragging on past the point of sanity. Even the courses he normally enjoyed, like arithmetics, were interminable and mind-numbing. Like a dark cloud was hanging over his shoulder, just waiting to release its downpour of rain.

When his final lesson of the day had concluded, Levi packed up his things and walked with Glenn outside. They talked for a while about how they thought the exam went until Glenn eventually bid him farewell and headed back toward his farm. Levi turned to the schoolhouse, watching the students filter out one by one. Austin should've been close behind him, but he was nowhere to be seen. It wasn't like him to be late. Usually, he leapt out of his chair and was first out the door when class was dismissed. Levi figured he must've stayed behind to talk with a friend, too.

Several minutes later, he did recognize a student leaving the schoolhouse, though it wasn't his brother. It was Jed, a boy around Austin's age. As soon as the brown-haired lug strolled down the steps with a leering smirk on his face, Levi knew something had gone down. Jed's older brother, Amos, followed a few steps behind, chuckling under his breath. No way two kids come out of their lessons looking that pleased with themselves unless they caused some trouble. What made Levi even more concerned was the fact that when the pair saw him, their grins grew even wider. They didn't say a word, though, while they walked past Levi and made their way toward the main street in town. Levi frowned, watching them saunter away.

"Christ Almighty," he muttered. He had a few ideas as to what could have occurred to bring so much joy to the boys and none of them were good.

That being said, he wasn't all that surprised when Austin emerged a few minutes later, long after the other students had left the building. His head was down, shoulders slumped. He was silent as he passed Levi, headed in the direction of the farm.

"Hey." Levi jogged a few steps to catch up and grabbed Austin by the shoulder. "Show me your face."

"No," muttered Austin, twisting his body away from his older brother.

"Show me."

A few seconds passed. Then, the boy released a breath and lifted his head.

"Another black eye?" Levi rolled his eyes. "Why do you keep lettin' them do this to you?"

"I'm not *lettin' them* do anythin'," Austin sneered. He took off walking again and Levi followed. "They were bad-mouthin' Ma again, sayin' she deserved what she got. I pushed one and told 'em all to go to hell, and Jed jumped me."

"Don't give 'em the time of day, Aus. Any kid who makes fun of another kid's dead Ma is just an ass."

Austin threw a glance toward Levi. "I did manage to get a few hits in. Besides, I get a chance to redeem myself tonight."

Levi narrowed his eyes. "Whaddya mean?"

"We're fightin' for real tonight, down in front of the school-house. At midnight. No more pussyfootin', no more screwin' around. Just the three of us on the dirt."

His older brother grabbed the strap of his rucksack and pulled him to a stop. "Aus, what're you thinkin'? That's a ridiculous idea."

The boy shrugged out of Levi's grip and crossed his arms. "What makes you so sure? I can hold my own."

"There's two of them against one of you. And you really agreed to that?"

Austin paused before replying slowly, "It was... kinda my idea." Levi sighed exasperatedly and Austin added, "Listen, maybe it wasn't the best idea. But I gotta stick up for myself, prove I can handle them."

"Gettin' yourself beat to a pulp in the middle of the night ain't gonna prove nothin'."

Austin dropped his head. "Well," he sighed, "what am I supposed to do now? If I don't show, they're gonna think I'm a sissy."

Levi closed his eyes. He knew what he had to do, but he *really* didn't want to do it. When he opened them, he found Austin staring at him with large, uncertain eyes. The older brother forced a grim smile to his face as he made his final choice. "I'll come with you. That way it's two on two, an even fight."

Austin grinned, wincing as he squinted his bruised eye. "You'd do that?"

"Yeah," Levi shrugged. "I can't let my little brother get his ass whooped by a couple of low-life bootlickers."

Austin smiled sheepishly. "Thanks, I guess."

His older brother put a hand on his shoulder and continued the walk toward home. "Don't thank me yet. I still have to make sure we come out of this in one piece."

Levi tried to remain cool and confident around Austin for the rest of the evening, but in actuality, he was terrified about the upcoming ordeal. He had only been in a handful of fights during his fifteen years of life thus far, and he wouldn't exactly call them enjoyable experiences. Between the two of them, Austin was always the one getting in skirmishes. Usually he came out relatively unharmed, but in the past few instances, it seemed like he was returning home with worse and worse injuries. Austin's classmates were starting to hit their growth spurts and the boy just couldn't keep up. Hopefully, if Levi was able to knock a bit of sense into the pair, they'd leave his brother alone once and for all. He wasn't worried about himself, since Levi could take Jed easily. Amos was a bit stockier and might be able to overpower Levi, but he'd just have to outsmart him. Having Austin there made things more complicated since Levi would not just have to worry about himself, but also his brother. Levi tried not to ponder it too much as they stepped onto the front porch.

Pa eyed up Austin's black eye when they got back, but he didn't mention it. He had already given them the "if you come back hurt, make sure they look worse" talk when they were kids. He also admitted that he had thrown a few punches when he was in common school, so as long as no one was ending up in the doctor's for the night, he wouldn't pry.

Levi cooked his usual dinner for the family and practiced his penmanship for a while until Pa declared it was time for bed. The two brothers headed upstairs obediently, following their nightly routine like they were also preparing for sleep. But every few minutes, they exchanged knowing glances. Neither would be getting much rest tonight.

By the time Levi was lying in bed, his heart was ready to pound out of his chest. His mind ran rampant with scenarios of how the night could fare, what could happen to him, or worse, to Austin. What felt like only a few minutes of scattered, frantic thoughts passed before he heard his bedroom door creak open. He looked up to see the silhouette of Austin in the doorway.

It was time.

The pair crept down the stairs, ensuring they could hear their father's beast-like snores coming from his bedroom, and snuck out the front door. They walked silently down the street, the only accompaniment to their thoughts being the crunch of the dirt beneath their work-worn boots. Levi looked over his shoulder to see the outline of the house slowly fading into darkness.

Suddenly, a wave of unease washed over him. Not the nervous adrenaline that usually preceded a fight, but another type of fear. Like his body was trying to tell him something his mind hadn't processed yet. He shoved it down and forced himself to steady his breathing. There was no time for fear. He had to focus.

The moon that normally provided a bit of light during the dark nights was shrouded by a blanket of clouds, dulling its glow. Levi had to squint to make out the shapes of the buildings and homes around them. Luckily, they had trodden the path into town many times, so the lack of light was only a minor hindrance.

"Levi?" Austin asked quietly.

"What?" his brother whispered back.

"What if they bring knives?"

Levi was glad Austin couldn't see his expression shift. "They won't bring knives. They ain't that low." He hoped he sounded convincing, but before Austin could reply, a rustle came from a bush on the opposite side of the road. The pair froze, staring at the location of the noise.

"Is it them?" Austin whispered.

"I don't think so," Levi breathed. "They live on the other side of town, and we're nowhere near the schoolhouse."

As he finished speaking, Levi clamped his mouth shut when a chill traced itself up his spine. His gaze swept across the street in front of him, searching for anything that would explain his sense of foreboding. Although he found nothing out of the ordinary, his mind was certain of one thing: someone, or something, was watching them.

It suddenly dawned on him that this sensation felt familiar. He had experienced the same thing just yesterday. In the woods, when Austin grabbed the pelt.

Another rustle sounded from the other side of the street. Levi turned toward it and he swore he saw a shadow duck behind the barn.

The breath evaporated from his lungs. His heart pounded in his ears as he stared with wide eyes where the movement had been. The darkness of the night seemed to ebb in front of his eyes, conjuring shapes in midair. It was possible it was just a trick of his mind, putting a physical presence to his subconscious fear.

Or it was possible there was something lurking there, blending in with the shadows.

The boy took a breath to steady himself. "We're goin' home." He spun on his heels and began striding in the opposite direction, sure that Austin would feel the same. But he was clearly mistaken.

"What?" Austin sprinted so he was in front of Levi, stopping him in his tracks. His older brother tried to maneuver around him, but the younger wouldn't budge. "Where're you goin'? You're givin' up already?"

Levi looked over his shoulder, back toward the town. The hairs on the nape of his neck were tingling, like something was breathing down his back. It was clear that his brother was not experiencing the same intuition he was. But he needed a reason they couldn't go any further. And he needed one now.

"Pa always said it's best to keep your head, right?" Levi replied, speaking quickly but evenly. Austin nodded. "Goin' out there and fightin' ain't the way to fix this. Just… go up to them tomorrow and talk it through. Like men. I'll come with you. But this ain't the way to resolve this."

Austin made a face. "You sure? They're gonna think I'm too scared to fight."

"That's better than disappointin' Pa." *Or ending up like Caroline and Ryder.* He put two hands on Austin's shoulders and spun him around. "Let's go, before he finds out we've gone."

Despite the fact that the pair were now headed away from the danger Levi had sensed, the feeling never relented. Even when they were back in the house and behind a locked door, it was as if the presence had followed him home. He tossed and turned for hours, willing his mind to calm and the chill to recede.

Though Levi laid in bed for many hours, sleep never found him.

When the rooster finally crowed to signal daybreak, Levi had just started dozing off. He slowly sat up and groaned as his head pounded painfully. The feeling of unease had finally dissipated and was replaced with utter exhaustion. Austin, on the other hand, seemed to have had no problem resting after the near-fight the previous night. Levi groggily made his way down the stairs, finding Austin already up and fully dressed, chowing down on a bowl of oats. He made eye contact with his brother and Austin gave him a small smile by way of greeting before putting his attention back on his breakfast.

"Hell, Levi." The boy turned to look at his father, who was standing at the wash bucket on the counter, scrubbing grime off his hands. Pa looked him over top-to-bottom. "You look like death."

"Didn't sleep well," muttered the boy, pouring himself a glass of water from the pail on the side table. He drank it down quickly and glanced at the clock on the wall next to the front door. "Aus, we gotta go."

Austin quickly shoved another two spoonfuls into his mouth, stood up, tossed his bowl in the dirty wash bin, and grabbed his rucksack off the back of his chair. Levi snagged his own bag off a hook on the kitchen wall and followed him. His brother was oddly obedient – maybe the incident yesterday had scared some sense into him. "'Bye, Pa," Levi called over his shoulder and shut the door behind him.

Although Austin had seemed mostly calm while eating breakfast, his anxious energy grew as they approached the schoolhouse. "Do you think they're gonna be mad I didn't show?" he asked.

"Maybe," replied Levi evenly. "But who cares?"

"Do you think they'll wanna do it another day?"

"If they do, tell 'em no. You're gonna handle this like an adult."

"But what if they *insist* we fight?"

"They can't fight someone who don't show up."

The younger brother gathered this was the end of the

conversation and remained silent the rest of the walk. When they turned the final corner, Levi noticed a crowd gathered outside the front steps. He recognized most of his classmates, but instead of the usual friendly chatter he expected to hear from his peers, a dull murmuring emanated from the group. One of the students saw them approaching and immediately stopped their conversation to stare. Within seconds, all of the kids had their attention on the brothers. Levi couldn't quite translate their expressions. They seemed mostly curious, but some had something darker in their eyes.

The pair paused a few feet away from the crowd. Austin leaned over to Levi. "Did somethin' happen?"

The older brother shook his head. "I dunno."

Suddenly, one of the boys separated themselves from the crowd. It was Amos – but something wasn't right. The boy's eyes were red-rimmed, his hair in disarray. His steps forward were jolted, unsteady, almost animalistic.

"What the hell have you done?!" Amos screamed, lunging forward. Without thinking, Levi stepped in front and held out his arms to shield his brother. The boy stopped inches away. His fists were balled at his sides and Levi saw there were tears rolling down his cheeks. Amos was not one to cry, especially in front of others.

"Calm down, Amos," Levi said. He heard the words shaking as they left his mouth. "What're you talkin' about?"

Amos' expression collapsed and when he spoke, his voice was tight with tears. "Jed. What Austin did to Jed, you motherless bitch."

Levi chose to ignore the venomous insult and glanced over his shoulder. Austin looked just as confused and shocked as Levi felt. "Last night? We – he didn't go last night, he stayed home."

"Stop lyin'!" Amos stumbled a step backwards, his hands gripping his hair like he meant to tear it out of his head. "I found him on the ground, right where he told me to meet him. There was – so much blood…" The boy paused to close his eyes. When he opened them, they were filled with such unbridled rage that Levi instinctively took a step back. "Austin shredded him. Tore him to *pieces*. I'll kill you, I swear to Christ I'll *kill you both!*" Amos charged at the pair, but two classmates grabbed him by either arm and pulled him back. He crumpled to the ground, heaving sobs. More students swarmed around him and moments later, he was lost from sight.

Levi turned to Austin with wide eyes. "What was that?" he whispered.

Austin's face was pale. "Is… is Jed dead?"

Just then, Levi felt a hand on his shoulder. He looked up and found himself face-to-face with a man. He had sharp features, harsh eyes, and a thick beard coating the bottom half of his face. Levi had never been officially introduced, but he recognized him immediately.

Sheriff Williams.

"Austin, Levi," the man said. His expression was taut and cold. "I'm to escort you both home, immediately. You are not to return to the schoolhouse until this… incident is discussed."

Chapter Three

No words were exchanged on the walk back to the farm. Occasionally, Levi would glance at his brother to try to catch his eye, figure out what he was thinking. But Austin kept his head lowered, staring at the ground beneath his feet. He wanted to reassure his brother, tell him that they'd figure out whatever happened. But for fear of accidentally saying something he shouldn't in front of the sheriff, he stayed silent.

Their father was in the barn when they arrived, in the process of milking one of the older mothers in the herd, Ruth. They strode up to the entrance and once they were in earshot, the sheriff cleared his throat. Pa rocked back on the stool, leaning around the cow. Ruth also turned to look toward the visitors, albeit much more slowly. "Sheriff," Pa grunted, his eyes narrowing. "What seems to be the problem?"

"I need to speak with you, Clint."

"Can it wait? I'm in the middle of tendin' to Ruth."

"I'm afraid it cannot."

The father's face hardened. He stood and wiped his hands along the stains of his jeans. "Let's get inside, then. Can I offer you somethin' to drink?"

"No, thank you."

Once inside, Austin and Levi quickly sat at the kitchen table. Pa walked to stand behind his sons while the sheriff remained on the opposite side of the room. Williams spoke first.

"Jed Lawson is dead."

Levi felt the air leave his lungs. He almost hadn't believed Amos when he first said it, but being told by Williams suddenly made it much more real. Jed really was dead. But how?

Pa frowned. "Bill and Catherine's boy? That's a damn shame. What happened to him?"

Williams looked to the brothers with a cold stare. "That's what I'm hoping Levi and Austin can shed some light on."

Pa straightened as he realized the implication. "What makes you think my boys had anythin' to do with this?"

The sheriff's expression was unyielding. "Amos told me that Austin had challenged Jed and himself to a fight in the middle of the night, on school grounds."

Pa glanced toward his youngest son. Upon reading the guilt on his face, he asked, "Alright, so what? That's what eleven-year-old boys do, they tussle."

"I'm just telling you what I heard, Mr. Oakley. When Amos went to meet him there, he found Jed. He was dead when his brother arrived."

"Whatever happened," answered Pa sharply, "musta happened before my boys got there."

"Let's hear what they have to say on the matter."

There was a long silence. Levi glanced up and saw both men staring at him and his brother. Austin had his gaze fixed on his hands folded in his lap, his eyes wide as saucers. The older brother swallowed, realizing it was up to him to take the lead. "It – it's true that Austin was gonna meet with him last night. But I convinced him not to."

"He didn't leave the farm last night?"

"No – I mean, yes, we did. But we only got to the edge of town before I told Austin to head back."

"You were out with him last night, then."

"Well – yeah. But only for a few minutes."

Williams withdrew a notepad and pencil from his back pocket and began scribbling something down. Levi couldn't help but feel like he said something terribly wrong, even though he had no idea what. He looked to Pa for reassurance. The man had his lips pressed shut, his arms crossed in front of him. He seemed to be listening to Levi just as intently as the sheriff was.

"Why did you want him to turn around?" the man asked, eyes still fixed to the paper.

Because I felt like we weren't alone. "I told Austin to handle it like a man. And gettin' into a brawl ain't the way to do that. We decided he would just talk it over with them in class the next day."

"Did you see anything strange when you were walking? Or anything that caught your eye?"

"No," Levi said, and quickly added, "but somethin' strange did happen a few days ago. One of our cows, Caroline, got killed, and my friend Glenn's dog died, too. All in the middle of the night. Maybe whatever killed them killed Jed, too."

"And what do you think killed the cow and dog?"

"A bear, probably."

The sheriff stared at the boy with narrowed eyes. "Why do you think an animal did it?"

"Whatever it was ripped through our fence and dragged Caroline to the woods. I don't think any person is strong enough to do that.

And we saw tracks that looked like a bear's." Levi stood, pointing to the front door. "If you want, I can show you, they're just a few–"

Williams held up a hand. "That won't be necessary." Levi slowly lowered himself back into his chair. The man dipped his pencil toward Austin. "You've been awfully quiet."

The younger brother lifted his head. His words shook as they passed his lips. "E-everythin' Levi said is true," he said. "We don't got nothin' to do with this."

For a long moment, all were quiet. The sheriff kept his eyes on the youngest, almost like he was daring him to speak another word. But Austin kept his mouth shut. His cheeks seemed to lose more color with each second that passed.

"See?" Pa cut in. "They told you what you wanted. They weren't even there last night."

Williams paused to write a few more words on his notepad. Eventually, he said, "I'm not convinced."

Pa took a step toward the man, hands clenched at his sides. "Are you callin' my boys liars?"

"Not necessarily," the sheriff replied evenly, refusing to respond to the father's escalation in volume. "I'm just not convinced an animal did this. We'll need to conduct a full investigation before I can draw any conclusions."

"Stop wastin' our time." Something about the way their father said the words made the boys straighten in their seats. The man was stock-still, his eyes flashing dangerously. "You know exactly what did this."

The sheriff's expression sharpened. "We need to talk to some others in town, see if they saw anything around the time of the attack."

Pa's lips curled around his next words, "It's Eloise all over again and you know it."

Levi froze. Pa must've misspoken – there was no way any of this had to do with…

"Can I speak with you in private, Mr. Oakley?"

Without responding, Pa turned and briskly walked into the other room. Williams swiftly followed.

Levi and Austin shared a look. Their expressions both asked the same thing: *Why did Pa mention her?* Silently, they leaned back in their chairs toward where the adults had walked, straining to pick up what they were saying. Levi was only able to catch a few fragmented words and phrases.

what happened last time… dead… the woods…

After eight minutes according to the clock hanging on the wall, Pa and the sheriff returned to the kitchen. Their father was significantly less composed than he was earlier. His brow was now beaded with perspiration and his eyes were blinking slightly too frequently. Williams' demeanor remained calm, but a sort of rabid energy radiated off of him.

The sheriff cleared his throat and turned toward the boys. "The schoolhouse is closed until my investigation has concluded. I will let you know when you're allowed to return. Is that understood?" The two boys nodded slowly. "Good." The sheriff addressed Pa and gave him a knowing look. "We're in agreement?" The man was silent as he glared back at Williams with dark eyes.

When it was clear Williams wasn't getting a response, he tipped his hat and stepped toward the entrance. He opened the front door, but turned to the boys one last time before exiting. "If either of your memories become more useful, you know where to find me."

As soon as the door clicked shut, Levi looked to his father. "What happened with him, Pa? What'd you say?"

His father ignored him. Instead, he kept his gaze locked straight ahead, staring at what appeared to be nothing. After a minute, he said, "The two of you are not to go near the woods and not to leave the house past sunset. Do you understand?"

"Yes," Levi answered, "but why did–"

"No more questions," Pa snapped. The man turned away from the boys, storming upstairs. A moment later, the study door slammed shut.

Levi and Austin released a breath. Austin picked at his cuticles nervously, his brow furrowed. "The sheriff really thinks we did this?"

His brother shook his head. "I'm not sure. But we know we didn't, and that's what's important. It's gotta be the same animal that killed Caroline and Ryder, it's the only thing that makes sense." Levi let out a breath, the severity of the situation washing over him. What happened to Jed almost happened to the both of them. The strange, instinctual fear he had felt to make them turn around had evidently saved their lives.

Austin crossed his arms, almost like he was shielding himself. "Pa sure ain't happy with Williams."

Levi raised his gaze upward as if he could see his father through the ceiling above him. "Whatever he talked about with Williams seemed to rattle him." The boy narrowed his eyes. "I just don't understand how Ma has anythin' to do with what happened to Jed. She passed away years ago."

The two brothers were silent, their minds desperate to come to a conclusion, but also too scared to ponder what that conclusion might be. After a few seconds, Levi steeled himself and forced his mouth into a sort of smile. "Let's just keep to ourselves and trust Pa to sort this out." Austin nodded, but kept his head down. Levi reached out and lightly punched his brother's arm.

"Hey, we get to play hooky for a few days, right? That ain't half bad."

At last, Austin's eyes brightened. "Yeah, I guess that's good."

"It is. Now go upstairs and wash up while I fix us some grub."

Once his little brother was out of sight, Levi finally allowed himself to drop the confident facade and let his expression go slack. He rested his head in his hands, struggling to process everything he had just heard.

There had been people killed in town before – it was a small town, news traveled fast. But in previous cases, the perpetrator had been caught and brought to justice. There wasn't a person at fault here, though. Just a wild animal. So that's why they were going about this so strangely.

That's not what everyone believed, Levi realized. There were two suspects connected to all of this, or at least people the sheriff believed to be suspects. If the town really thought Levi and Austin were involved in all this, why didn't they just arrest them? Levi would've almost preferred that, so he could go to trial and clear his name faster.

Levi suddenly sat up when it dawned on him. Austin and him were kids, not adults. Only adults went to trial around here, he had never once heard of a kid going to trial for anything – especially not for murder.

They were keeping the two of them home until they decided what to do with them. Or worse – they found more evidence to prove their case.

The boy stood to get the loaf of bread from off the counter to prepare for lunch. That explained why Williams was acting the way he did: he was trying to decide if he had enough information to throw the boys in a cell. But that still didn't explain what all this had to do with their mother. And at the moment, it didn't seem like Pa was interested in sharing what he thought about all of this.

Regardless, he thought as he layered cheese onto rye, *there's no use worryin' now. Gotta trust that Pa will make things right.*

Once it was clear their father wasn't leaving his study in time for lunch, Levi and Austin started on their chores for the day. The boys knew their duties on the farm well enough to complete them without being told, even if they normally worked on them after their lessons. There was plenty to be done between feeding the herd, gathering the fresh supply of eggs, and preparing the butter and cheese from the day's supply of milk. It might've been Levi's mind playing tricks on him, but the animals seemed more jittery than usual. They stamped their feet impatiently, jumped at every little sound. Almost like they, too, could feel a tension looming over the farm.

As the hours passed, the sun swept across the sky and shadows stretched along the grass. When the last of the day's blue was overtaken by the scarlet of sunset, the boys retreated inside. Just as Levi was putting the finishing touches on supper, he heard the upstairs study door open. Plodding footfalls approached and Pa entered the kitchen. Levi wasn't sure what to expect in terms of his appearance, but he was surprised to find him quite put together. He had changed into a new set of clothes and had even taken the time to shave. Pa nodded to both his sons before sitting at the kitchen table. Levi and Austin exchanged looks, then followed suit.

They said grace in unison and started on supper. The boys kept their eyes firmly locked on their food, not daring to make eye contact with their father. But surprisingly, it was Pa who spoke first.

"Now," he started. Both Levi and Austin froze with their forks halfway to their mouths. They slowly looked up and rested their forks on the sides of their plates. Once Pa was sure he had their full attention, he cleared his throat and repeated, "Now, I wanna make one thing clear. This… time off from lessons ain't an excuse to slack-off."

The two sons nodded quickly.

Pa sat forward and continued, "I'll assign you both chores every mornin' and I expect them completed prior to supper. That's in addition to your usual chores as well. This comes at a good time, there's plenty to be done around the farm. I expect you both to pull your weight. Is that understood?" Again, the boys nodded.

"What're we gonna do about the bear?" asked Austin.

The man clenched his jaw. "We'll make the fence stronger, add more barbed wire. Like I told Levi."

"But how are we gonna defend ourselves if it comes back? What if it attacks one of us like it did Jed?"

"You'll have to worry about the people in town attackin' you before a bear does."

Austin looked to Levi, uncertain of how to respond. "Well," Levi said cautiously. "Can we use your guns to defend ourselves if someone comes after us?"

"Absolutely not."

"What're we gonna do, then? Just run away?" Levi took a breath, choosing his next words carefully. "We're not just gonna sit here and let our names get dragged through the mud because of some rumor. If the chance comes to defend ourselves, we have to take it."

"As your father," Pa said firmly, "it's my duty to protect you both. Anyone who comes after you is goin' to have to get through me first." The man was silent for a moment, then added, "However, if y'all are really concerned, I can teach you a few things. We can set aside an hour each day."

Austin squinted at him. "What kinda things?"

"Self-defense. How to protect yourselves – and attack, if the time is right." Pa's face darkened at his last words.

Austin and Levi both nodded. It wasn't quite what they had been hoping for, but if Pa was right about trouble heading their way, any help they got from their father would be better than nothing.

As Levi carefully inspected Pa's face, he caught a certain glint in his eye. It was one that made him sit back, made his eyes widen. He had only seen it one other time, many years ago. It scared him now, just as much as it had scared him then.

He glanced toward Austin to see if he had noticed it too. His little brother made eye contact with him before turning back toward their father. But the partial glance was enough for Levi to know the moment wasn't lost on him, either.

"Is all that clear?"

"Yessir," answered the sons.

"Good." Pa tore off a piece of meat from a bone and shoved it into his mouth. After chewing and swallowing, he said, "Straight to bed once you're both finished. We've got a long day ahead of us tomorrow."

The boys came down the stairs the following morning to find scraps of paper lying on the kitchen table. True to his word, Pa had written out schedules for each of them. He had outlined the entire day including thirty minutes set aside for meals, an hour for studies, and two extended blocks of time during which the extra chores around the farm were to be completed. There was also one hour of physical training immediately following lunch.

"Don't dawdle, now," the man said, handing each of the boys a plate of toast and eggs. "Finish your breakfast and head out there. I'll meet you in the barn."

The brothers scarfed down their meals, strapped on their boots and made their way outside. The sun had just begun to peak out over top of the far hill and the chill of crisp morning air danced on the boys' cheeks as they walked to the barn. Upon entering, they noticed two stools and two metal pails placed near the doorway. Pa was already sitting on a different stool under one of the cows and he gestured the boys over. "Go on," he said. "Grab a pail and a stool and get goin'."

Levi grabbed the supplies before sitting under the cow on his father's right. Austin did the same next to his older brother. They had been taught from the day they could walk how to tend to the cattle and Pa had always emphasized how important it was to milk them properly. Not only was it critical for their health, but it was also one of the best ways to bond with the herd. It showed the animals you could be trusted and identified you as a leader.

Levi held out his right hand and touched his thumb to his pointer finger. His father's words from years ago rang in his mind while he let muscle memory take over. *Wrap your hand around the top and feel the pocket of milk. Next, roll your fingers down the teat to squeeze it out.*

Soon enough, there were three pails filled with fresh milk. The boys spent the next few minutes milking the rest of the cows, bringing filled buckets to the house and returning for more. Next, they refilled the feeding troughs and gave them clean water. Pa seemed to have a never-ending list of tasks for the boys, from cleaning out the stables to brushing the family's mule, Samson.

Once Austin was occupied, Pa showed Levi how to reinforce the fence. He added a second layer of barbed wire to the top and stones to the bottom of the posts. After about three hours, the boys and their father were sweating and winded.

"Alright," Pa said, pursing his lips in what wasn't quite a smile, but was still an expression of approval. "Y'all did some good work this mornin'. Hurry inside now and do some readin'. And drink some water. I'll meet you there once it's time for lunch."

"Yessir," the boys replied and hurried inside, lest the man remember another task he forgot to assign them.

After the brothers each gulped down several glasses of water, they gathered their slate, chalk, and books. They sat on opposite ends of the kitchen table and splayed their work in front of them. Levi got right to work without hesitation, but Austin was less motivated. The younger brother glowered at his arithmetics book, then sighed and stared out the kitchen window.

"Do you wanna be a farmer when you're older?" Austin asked.

Levi looked up from his slate. "What?"

"That's all farmers do, what we were just doin'. Just milk cows and feed them and clean stuff."

Levi couldn't help but crack a smile. "Well, yeah. It's their job."

"And you want to do that? Forever?"

"Uh huh. It's our legacy, this farm has been in our family for generations."

The younger brother made a face. "I'm not sure I want to be a farmer."

"You want to keep doing arithmetics for the rest of your life?"

Levi replied, gesturing to the boy's open book. "'Cause that's all learned people do for their jobs. Just stare at numbers all day."

Austin rolled his eyes. "I don't even know why we gotta do this. It's Saturday."

"Better to be ahead than behind."

"I'd rather not be doin' it at all."

"Well, you can do that or clean out the manure in the barn. Your choice."

Austin pouted and hunched back into his work. A few seconds later, though, he raised his eyes again. "Levi?"

"Yeah?"

"You think…" he trailed off, rolling a pencil in his hand. "You think what happened to Jed is my fault?"

"What?" Levi's eyebrows shot up. "No way! We didn't even go to the schoolhouse."

"No, I mean–" Austin wouldn't meet his brother's gaze. "I was the one that asked them to fight that night. So, if he hadn't been there, maybe he wouldn't have…"

Levi quickly shook his head. "No, Aus, you can't think like that. If the bear was out at night, it didn't care who it was goin' after. If it weren't Jed, it woulda been someone else. Just like if it weren't Caroline on our farm, it woulda been another animal killed. They were both just at the wrong place at the wrong time. No way you coulda known somethin' like that was goin' happen."

A bit of peace seeped onto Austin's face, but he wasn't totally convinced. "I just couldn't tell what Pa was thinkin' last night. He was actin' strange."

The expression Levi had seen immediately flashed into his mind. "Well, he's clearly – angry about this whole situation."

"Not that." Although Austin seemed focused on his

schoolwork, Levi could see the distress and uncertainty lining his face. "He got a sort of look. Like, a scary look."

Levi dropped his head, hoping his brother didn't see the fear he knew was written on his own face. "Yeah, I saw."

"I ain't never seen him like that before."

I have. Levi almost said it aloud, but he stopped the words right on the tip of his tongue. He glanced up quickly, but Austin didn't seem to notice his brother's hesitation. Levi pretended to continue studying, randomly scanning his eyes along the page to feign reading. But he couldn't stop thinking about his father's vicious gaze. He had only seen it one other time throughout his life, but he remembered it well.

It was the day their mother died.

Levi's train of thought was broken by a smack on the kitchen window. Both brothers started and twisted their heads toward the sound. There was a yellow splotch on the pane, trickling downward. They exchanged a glance before running to the front door. Levi reached it first and swung it open. At first he didn't notice anything amiss, but then he saw movement down the road. A pair of boys were running away, faint laughter echoing behind them.

"Was that an egg?" asked Austin.

Levi looked toward the window and saw the fragments of white littering the ground and the yellow stain. "Yeah."

"Why'd they do that?"

Turning back to the retreating figures, Levi kept his gaze on them until they were out of sight. "Sheriff Williams may not be totally convinced that we were involved with Jed's death. But that don't mean the rest of the town agrees with him."

Austin furrowed his brow. "Oh."

Levi shook his head in disdain before gesturing to the egg splatter. "Go get a cloth and clean that up, wouldja?"

"Why don't you do it?"

"It's either that or back to arithmetics."

Austin thought for a moment, then snorted in annoyance and went inside to grab a dishrag. His older brother remained outside, staring at the place where the boys headed back into town. He couldn't let Austin see how scared he was of all of this. He had seen what the town was like when a man had been tried for murder a few years back. How they smiled and cheered as they watched the man swing from his neck until dead.

He understood the scope of what an angry town could do. And right now, that anger was directed straight at his family.

Chapter Four

L EVI FELT BOTH excited and slightly wary while he waited for Pa to start the self-defense lessons. Pa had never done anything like this with his sons and Levi was uncertain what he had in mind. Right when the hour hand touched twelve, Pa called for the brothers. The pair rose from their respective locations at the kitchen table and followed their father into the yard. As soon as they walked outside, Levi took note of two grain sacks propped up in the middle of the field.

Once they were close enough, Pa pointed to the two mounds of burlap. Levi and Austin each set up across from a grain sack. Austin glanced back and forth between the sack and his father. Levi noticed he was picking at his nails.

"Alright," grunted Pa. "Each of you throw a punch." The boys hesitated. "Now."

Levi looked expectantly toward his brother, but Austin only stared back at him anxiously. It was clear he wasn't going first. Rolling his eyes, Levi squared up toward the grain. He closed his fists, holding out both in front of him. He needed to show Pa he wasn't the scrawny kid he used to be. Levi took a moment to steady his breath, then threw his fist forward.

Instantly, a searing pain raced up his forearm. He leapt back, clutching his arm and gritting his teeth. After he realized what he had done, he forced his face back into a neutral expression and dropped his hands to his sides. When he looked at Pa, the man's face was unsurprised. The father's gaze turned to Austin. "And you."

The younger brother's eyes widened even further and he looked to Levi for support. His brother only stared back at him with a dull look. Austin also raised his fists, though slightly more timidly. His fist hit the burlap and he instantly let out a hiss, grabbing his hand.

Levi's gaze dropped to his feet. He thought he and his brother were a bit more savvy when it came to combat. But they couldn't even throw a decent hit against a sack of grain. How were they supposed to protect themselves?

When he glanced up at Pa, however, his father's expression was kind. "I know you two will hold your own out there if it comes down to it," Pa said to his sons. "But you've got to brush up on the basics so you don't end up gettin' hurt. Or worse, end up hurtin' yourselves. Like you both just did. I'll teach you, as long as you're both willin' to learn. Are you willin' to learn?"

Levi and Austin didn't have to look to each other for support before giving their answers. "Yessir."

"Good." Pa walked over to his sons and wrapped a hand around each of their dominant arms. "Throwin' a good punch starts with the point of contact: your fist. If your fist ain't prepared to take the brunt of the impact, you either won't have as much power as you want, or it'll hurt like hell. I'd guess the two of you experienced the second?" After receiving nods of confirmation, Pa raised his right fist. "Raise your hand up." He then curled four of his fingers downward and left his thumb outstretched. "Roll down your fingers, like this. This should be your instinctive first step when you're makin' a fist. Tuck your thumb in first and you're liable to break your wrist. You gotta wrap your thumb 'round the outside of your other fingers. Make sure it rests against your pointer and middle fingers. Don't have it go too far down or too far out." He modeled the motions for the boys and pointed to the two of them with his opposite hand. "You try."

Glancing back and forth between their father's hand and their own, the boys repeated the motions. Pa inspected each of their fists, making slight adjustments as needed. Once he was satisfied, he held up his own fist again. "Where you make contact is also important. You gotta make sure your hit lands on the knuckles of your top and middle fingers. That's the strongest and hardest part of your hand, so it can take the most impact." Pa stepped back, gesturing to the grain sacks. "Keep your fist like it is and try again." There were two thuds of crunching grain. "Good. Again."

The boys each took turns throwing punches. Levi was amazed at how just a few changes could reduce the pain he felt to a dull ache. It was still there, but it was much more manageable. Austin and Levi also seemed to be hitting stronger, too, as the sound grew louder with each contact.

"Excellent, Levi. Keep your feet apart, Aus. There ya go. Make sure you're drivin' your left arm in while you're throwin' with your right. Perfect. C'mon, Levi, gimme a little more power, I know you got it in you. There ya go."

This continued for several minutes until Pa finally said, "Alright, that's enough, boys." The brothers stepped back, their breathing labored. Levi rolled his shoulders back, already feeling a tightness from the exertion. "Yeah, make sure you two stretch those arms. We're gonna be doin' a lot more of this in the comin' days."

"Yessir," said the brothers in unison.

When Levi met Pa's eyes, he saw a brightness in them that hadn't been there yesterday. Maybe Pa wasn't as lost as he had feared in that moment with Williams.

But just as suddenly as Levi had noticed it, the look faded. The lines of age and pain once again carved the man's expression and his eyes darkened.

"I'll let you two off easy the first day. Get some water and wash up," Pa said, tipping his hat and striding back toward the farmhouse. "I expect supper on the table at six sharp, Levi."

The boy pursed his lips, steeling himself before following his father. "Yessir."

The next morning, the brothers came downstairs to find Pa at the kitchen table, a cup of coffee already sitting in front of him. They quietly put together plates of food for themselves and sat across from their father. As they started eating, Levi couldn't help but notice the uncomfortable silence hanging in the air. Neither Pa nor Austin were the most talkative in the morning, though they usually were polite enough to exchange a few words of greeting. When Levi glanced up, he found Pa staring blankly across the room. Deep bags hung under his eyes and his chin was layered in dark scruff. Levi watched for several seconds and the man didn't seem to blink.

Suddenly, Pa stood. Austin and Levi jumped, but Pa wasn't focused on them. Instead, his gaze seemed unfocused, like his mind was miles away.

"Your schedules are on the table," the man said. Without looking at his sons, he strode across the room and up the stairs.

The brothers winced when his study door shut.

Levi picked up one of the pieces of paper laid before them.

"Looks the same as yesterday," he muttered. "I guess he expects us to do our chores ourselves and he'll meet us for fight lessons."

Grabbing the other paper, Austin said, "There's more chores than yesterday."

When Levi saw Austin's disparaging face, he added, "Hey, finish your breakfast and let's get goin'. The quicker we start, the quicker we'll be done with 'em." The younger brother nodded his agreement, dropped the paper, and continued with breakfast.

After some more coaxing from Levi, both brothers eventually made their way into the yard. They completed their usual chores and lessons in the morning, albeit a bit slower than the previous day since they had one less set of hands. Their father joined them for a silent lunch and retreated back upstairs during the boys' free time. While Austin spent the hour carving a shiv out of a scrap of firewood, Levi decided to read a book on the front porch. He stationed himself on the outside of the house, his back against a wall and his feet facing the road on the way into town.

A few minutes later, the boy felt the hairs prick up on the back of his neck. He raised his head slowly to not garner suspicion and scanned the property. It appeared empty. But his gut told him something wasn't right. Though he lowered his head back down toward his book, his eyes remained up and keenly observing.

There. A dark shadow flitted behind the barn.

Levi quietly closed the book and set it on the ground. He rose to his feet while his heart began to race. Ever since the night of the incident with Jed, he kept his knife on him. He was thankful for it now as he pulled it from his pants pocket, snapped it open, and slowly began walking toward the barn.

Levi kept his eyes wide, daring the shadow to move again. But from what he could see, it seemed to stay behind the far wall.

The knife grew slick in his hand and he tightened his grip. He only had one chance to surprise whoever this was.

Once he reached the building, Levi pressed his back against the wall adjacent to the one he had seen the shadow dart behind. He once again adjusted the knife in his hand, breathing deeply.

Levi shut his eyes, took a breath. Then, he spun around the corner with the knife raised.

A person was there, short and stocky, their back to Levi. When they turned around to see the boy and his knife, they backed away with their hands raised. "Levi," he hissed. "It's me!"

Levi dropped his hand to his side. "Glenn? What're you doin' here?"

Glenn let his hands fall as well, heaving a sigh of relief. "I came to see how you're doin'. After Friday and all."

"I'm fine. We're all fine." Levi glanced back toward the house to see if Pa had spotted the intruder. For now, the house was quiet. Usually Pa was fine with visitors, but in the state he was in, Levi couldn't be sure. Much as Levi was relieved to see his friend, he couldn't help but feel that they shouldn't be seen together. If the town was wary of the Oakely family, the last thing he wanted was his friend to get tied up in suspicion, too. "Look, it's good to see you and all, but I don't think you should be here right now."

"I know," Glenn said quickly. "But I just had to know what Williams said to you. Rumor is the sheriff thinks you and Austin killed Jed."

Levi winced. "Well, not exactly, but it's not far off. He thinks we were somehow involved."

"How come?"

"Austin challenged Jed and Amos to a fight that night." Levi rolled his eyes, realizing how childish it seemed after everything that had happened. "I started to walk with him to the schoolhouse so it would be an even fight, two on two, but I convinced him to turn back before we got to the school. Amos found Jed there and thought it musta been Austin that did him in."

"So, you never actually got to the schoolhouse."

"Uh huh. But just the fact that we were *supposed* to be there is apparently enough to make us suspects."

Glenn shook his head. "If anythin', it's probably the bear that killed Caroline and Ryder."

A wave of relief washed over Levi. "Yes, exactly." He threw another look toward the house, his anxiety regarding his father's whereabouts growing by the second. "If that's all you're here to ask about, I think you best be goin'."

"That's not quite all." Glenn took a step closer to the boy and lowered his voice. "I also came to warn you."

Levi narrowed his eyes. "Warn me 'bout what?"

Glenn flicked his gaze back toward the road headed into town. Like he was looking for someone. "Amos hasn't… been well since his brother died. He wandered around town all day yesterday. I even saw him out again early this mornin', I'm not sure he ever went to sleep. He's mutterin' to himself, wringin' his hands. And – I heard him mention yours and Aus' names."

"You think he's gonna do somethin'?"

"I don't think so, at least not now. I heard the sheriff was gonna talk to his Ma, keep him home until he's more stable. Besides, the sheriff and a few other men in town started patrollin' the streets at night, lookin' for anythin' strange. I'm sure they'd send him home if they saw him out at night."

"Did they see anythin' last night?"

"Not that I heard. But they'll be goin' out again tonight." Glenn hesitated before adding, "I did hear a lot of kids in town aren't happy with your family. After you left, they were sayin' some awfully nasty things."

"They can't seriously believe Austin or I would do somethin' like this."

"It's more that they don't like the fact that y'all are associated with what happened. And right now, there's no other suspects."

"They're lookin' for the wrong thing. They should be lookin' for an animal, not us."

"I know that. But the rest of them don't, and they want someone to blame."

Levi pointed to the far window of the house. "Someone egged the house yesterday. Pair of kids, saw 'em runnin' back down the hill. Any idea who mighta done it?"

Glenn heaved a sigh. "Probably Cole and Jesse. When you and Aus left yesterday, they talked about it non-stop for at least an hour. Honestly, they'll probably come for you before Amos does."

"Well, that's great to hear."

"Hey, listen." Glenn put a hand on Levi's shoulder. "I'll do what needs to be done to get those kids to leave you alone. Rough 'em up, if I have to."

"Don't do that," Levi replied quickly. "Things are bad enough, don't make it worse."

"If it means them leavin' you and your family alone, I'll do what needs to be done." Glenn's eyes darkened. "I'm not scared of Williams and his ruffians. But neither are Cole and Jesse. Besides, you saw what Jed and Amos did to Aus just for kicks. Imagine what the boys'll do when there's a motive behind the punches."

"We can hold our own."

"True. But wouldn't it be nice to have someone else on your side?"

To that, Levi had no response. He mulled it over for a

moment and said, "Do what you want. We appreciate the help, but it ain't necessary. It's more helpful for you to be our ear in town, let us know what people are sayin' when we're not around."

Glenn dropped his hand. "I can do that, no problem. But just know I'll be there for you if you need me to be." His expression quickly wilted as he changed the subject. "What did your Pa say about all this?"

"He was pretty angry with Williams, since he was basically callin' Austin and me liars." When he remembered, he added, "Pa said somethin' weird, too. He mentioned Ma by name, like she was somehow related to all this."

Glenn raised his eyebrows. "That's mighty strange. What's she got to do with anythin'?"

"He didn't say. At least, not to Austin and me. But I honestly don't remember much of what happened the night she passed, and Pa never talks about it."

Glenn was quiet as he bit his lip thoughtfully. "You think there would be anythin' about that in the library? Like a newspaper article or somethin' we could look into? If your Pa ain't gonna talk about what really happened to your Ma, we might be able to find some information on it ourselves." He paused, giving Levi a look. "I mean, if you're alright readin' about that sorta thing."

Although Levi tried to push the thought of the day to the back of his mind, a trickle of memories pushed forward. He saw his mother's limp body in his father's arms. The vacant look on Pa's face. His mother's dress, painted red with blood.

Levi blinked and quickly nodded. "I'm fine," he said. "It's worth lookin' into. I remember seein' an article posted in the paper, but I – never read it." He didn't think Glenn needed to know that Pa had hidden everything in the house that had to do with their mother, so even if he had wanted to, he wouldn't have been able to find it. If one walked into the Oakley household today, it would seem as if the woman never existed.

Glenn studied Levi's face like he could glimpse the struggle behind the boy's eyes. "If you want, I could look at it myself and tell you what I find. I'd just need to know the date."

"No," Levi replied firmly, mentally shaking himself. He needed to focus. "I'll come with you. Though I dunno how I'd get there. I'm too busy on the farm durin' the day and Pa won't let us off the property at night."

"It's easier to sneak out at night than durin' the day."

"But that's exactly how Jed got killed. And there's gonna be people patrollin'."

"We'll be careful," Glenn replied. "Jed didn't know there was somethin' to be scared of. We do, so we'll be ready for it if it comes. I'll meet you on your property at midnight tonight. We'll sneak inside the library, get our article, and get out. No problem."

"I dunno…" The memory of the chill ached in the back of Levi's mind. He considered trying to explain it to Glenn, how he was pretty sure it saved his and his brother's life… but how could he? Explaining to his friend his mysterious intuition without sounding crazy seemed impossible. "What if the bear comes back?"

Glenn shrugged. "I can bring my Pa's gun and we can blow it away."

"He'll let you borrow it?"

"Yours don't let you borrow his?"

"Not unless he's with us. He treats them all like his second set of children."

"Hm. Well, my Pa is fine with it. He even said yesterday after the whole thing happened with Jed, whenever I'm out at night he wants it on me."

Levi thought for a moment, torn by his desire to please his

father, his curiosity about the truth – and his fear of the mysterious killer in Ainsworth. But more than anything, he wanted to know what any of this had to do with his mother. If he was being honest with himself, he had wondered about the day of her death long before Jed died. This might just be his opportunity to discover what (if anything) his father had hidden from him about that day. "We'll move fast," he relented and Glenn pumped his fist. "No longer than five minutes inside. I know exactly what date we're lookin' for."

"Deal," Glenn said. He gestured to Levi's knife. "Oh, also – you might want to look into an upgrade if your Pa ain't gonna let you use his gun."

Levi examined the knife in his hands. His friend was right. Based on what this creature did to Caroline, no knife was gonna slow it down. He needed something better, stronger. And if Pa wasn't going to allow him to be properly protected, he would have to take care of it himself.

"You got a point. I'll work on scroungin' up some cash." Putting out his hand, Levi said, "Thanks for stoppin' by, Glenn. Be safe, alright?"

Glenn shook it and replied, "You too. See ya tonight."

"See ya."

With a nod of his head, Glenn looked once more toward the farm house before sprinting toward the back fence. He ducked his head down, tracing along the edge until he was out of sight and headed back toward town.

So that's how he made it onto the property without being seen, Levi thought as he walked back toward the house. He had to be more careful about keeping track of who was on the property. Luckily, Glenn was a welcome visitor. There were many from town that wouldn't be.

As Levi laid in his cot, staring at the ceiling once again, he couldn't help but feel like he was repeating history after what had happened only days before. Just like that night, he was counting down the minutes, waiting for the right moment to sneak off into town without his father's knowledge. He was afraid now, too, but for very different reasons than he had been afraid then. He hoped his subconscious was accurate enough to warn him again if there was impending danger, whether it be the boys from the schoolhouse or whatever else could be found in the shadows.

Once it was midnight according to the clock on his bedroom wall, Levi peeked outside his window. Right on schedule, there was a shadow sneaking around the edge of the fence, the same path Glenn had followed earlier that day. Levi crept downstairs, laced up his shoes, and strode into the night. The moon was only half-lit, casting an eerie glow on the property. He had just enough to see by as he made his way across the field.

Levi turned the corner of the barn wall and found Glenn's face grinning back at him. "I'm surprised you showed up," Glenn whispered, lightly punching his friend's arm. "I thought for sure you'd chicken out. Your Pa is way more scary than whatever bear or coyote is lurkin' 'round here."

Levi ignored the comment and instead asked, "You got the gun?"

Glenn turned sideways to show the rifle slung over his shoulder. "Loaded and ready."

"Let's move."

The two boys strode around the back of the farm, moving quickly and quietly. Once they reached the edge of the fence, they jogged the perimeter of the property until they were out of sight of the house. Only then did they allow themselves to slow their pace and step onto the dirt road. It reminded Levi of when he and Glenn used to scurry out at night when they were eight or nine. In their youth, they would tiptoe around Ainsworth playing hide-and-seek, chasing any animals they saw, and struggling to quiet their laughter. Those late night excursions were some of Levi's favorite childhood memories. But their playful, buoyant skipping from years ago was a stark contrast to the cautious slinking of this night.

Levi kept waiting for that familiar sinking feeling to start, that chilled his bones and stifled his breath. In spite of his pumping heart and twitching hands, however, the night remained quite peaceful. A light breeze floated through the town, bringing with it the smell of fresh daisies. Spring was just beginning to melt into summer and the flowers in the neighboring gardens peaked their faces out from their darling buds. During the day, the gardens were painted in brilliant color. In the dead of night, however, they were diluted into hues of blue and black.

Right as they made the final turn onto the street, Glenn suddenly shot out an arm in front of Levi. Levi made a face and prepared to object, but Glenn put a finger to his lips. That's when Levi saw him.

A few hundred feet in front of them, across from the library, was a man. He held a lit cigar between his lips and from the flickering light at the end, they could see he was around middle-aged. Not the sheriff or someone instantly recognizable, but Levi was pretty sure he had seen him dropping off one of their classmates in front of the schoolhouse. Probably the father of a student in their class.

Clasped loosely in his hands was a hunting rifle.

The man strolled forward slowly, head twisting from left to

right as he scanned the street. When he began to move his gaze in the direction of the boys, Levi and Glenn ducked behind the closest building.

"We've gotta distract him," breathed Levi.

Glenn nodded, a hint of a smile dancing on his lips. It was clear the thrill of doing something they weren't supposed to was outweighing the fear of getting caught.

Levi inspected the ground, then picked up a shot glass-sized rock lying at their feet. He carefully tilted his head around the corner, just far enough so he could see the man's location. He was no more than twenty feet away from where they were hiding. They had to act now.

Taking a breath, Levi stepped away from the wall and pivoted to face it. He gripped the rock in his right hand, aimed above the roof, and launched it with all his strength.

The stone careened through the air and the pair quickly lost sight of it in the hazy light. They heard it land on a neighboring roof before tumbling down to the ground.

From the other side of the building, the man let out a disgruntled huff. Levi heard his shuffling steps retreating toward where the rock had landed.

"Now," Levi whispered.

Levi and Glenn scampered toward the library, careful not to drag their feet. Levi's first thought was to try the front door, but he knew that was almost certainly locked. Instead, he headed toward the nearest window on the side of the building. He gripped the bottom of the frame and shoved upwards. It didn't budge.

"Damn," he cursed under his breath, stealing a look toward the man. His back was to them, glancing from side to side. It was only a matter of time before he turned their way.

Glenn gestured toward his friend and the two of them raced

around the other side of the library. Here, at least, they were concealed from the man's view. But they still had to move quickly, lest he decide to investigate the area further. Glenn stepped up to the next window and, to their surprise, it glided open. They exchanged triumphant grins and grasped the windowsill, peering inside the building.

There was no sign of any patron present, or the husband and wife that owned it. Although Levi successfully made it inside without causing too much of a ruckus, Glenn ended up knocking over a stack of history books with his foot. The two froze, waiting with bated breath to see if the man outside had heard. After a few seconds of tense silence, Levi sighed in relief and annoyance, then socked Glenn in the arm.

"Sorry," his friend hissed apologetically as he helped Levi gather the scattered books.

Once all was back in its original place, Levi pointed to the back left corner of the building. "That's where they keep their newspaper records. I heard they've got copies datin' back to when the town was established, so they gotta have somethin' from a few years ago."

Glenn glanced at his friend as they wove in and out of the bookshelves. "How do you know all this?"

"I... kinda come here a lot."

The library was owned by an elderly couple who had established the place when they got married. The wife liked Levi and always recommended new books for him. Her husband felt differently and seemed to hold a grudge against him ever since he dog-eared a copy of *The Odyssey* several months back. But that never stopped Levi from returning and trading in old stories for new ones every few weeks.

Just as Levi had described, the back corner was piled high

with crates. Each held dozens of newspapers stacked together and bound by twine. The outside of the crates were marked with neat writing that detailed the two months and year each one contained.

"What're we lookin' for?" Glenn asked while he scanned the dates.

"April 19th, 1871."

After a few moments, his friend pointed to the third row from the left. "There. March through April, '71."

There were only two crates stacked on top of the one they needed and they had little problem lowering them to the ground. Levi cut off the twine using his pocketknife and the boys started searching. They made it through a couple dozen papers before Levi paused. "Wait a minute." He held up two newspapers side-by-side. His eyes flicked back and forth between them. "That don't make sense."

Glenn looked over his shoulder and read the dates aloud. "April 19th and… April 21st?"

Levi sat back on his haunches. "It's missin'. The paper with the article ain't here."

"Well, didn't she die on the 19th? Wouldn't the article be in that paper?"

"It takes time to write somethin' like that, it don't just get posted right away the day it happens. I remember it bein' the front page of the followin' day." He flipped through the April 21st edition and added, "I don't see anythin' about it in here. Which means it must've been on the 20th."

This made things much more complicated. Not only did it seem like Pa was trying to hide something about Ma's death, but it seemed like the town was, too. Levi's stomach dropped as the reality of it all set in. He had been right. There *was* something strange about the day Ma died. He had always thought Pa's reasoning for reducing her presence in their home to mere memory was because the reminder of her was too painful. But this was the proof he had been looking for that Pa wasn't being entirely honest.

The paper must have been taken by someone. But why? Why *that* day? Was it really something to do with Ma's passing? Or did something else happen on that day besides the tragedy? Something related to what killed Jed? It was possibly overlooked by Levi with everything that had happened those years ago, but he wasn't convinced. If it was that important, how come he hadn't heard of it before?

"Wait a minute." Glenn interrupted Levi's thoughts. "Look at this."

Levi turned his attention to where Glenn was motioning. *"Clint Oakley arrested for misconduct and assault?"*

"It's dated the week followin' your Ma's passin', on the 30th." Glenn skimmed a few lines. "Don't say any more than that. Do you remember your Pa gettin' arrested?"

Levi was silent as he thought back. "I do remember Pa leavin' us home alone for an evenin', pretty soon after Ma was killed."

His mind flashed with the image of his brother seated across from him at the dinner table, plain bread and cheese on their plates. Levi sitting by the window until the night stars bled into sunrise, waiting for his father to come home. Waking up with his forehead pressed into the glass, fear gripping his core as he realized his father hadn't yet returned.

When his father finally arrived several hours later, the man was silent. His eyes were wide, his hair ungroomed. He had walked into the barn and started working without a word to his sons. They never spoke of that day. Levi had almost entirely buried the memory until that very moment.

"He came home the next mornin'," Levi said softly. "It's possible it had to do with his arrest. But I feel like he woulda been kept in jail longer for a thing like that, no? He was only gone for a night."

"Dunno. Think you could ask him?"

"That'll go over well. How would I even explain what we were doin' in the library? Or why I left the farm when he specifically told me not to?"

Glenn winced. "True." The usual mirth in his face was clouded with unease. "Well, now we know one thing for certain. We're not the only ones concerned about what happened to your Ma. Either someone is tryin' to take the information for themselves, or they're tryin' to hide it."

The two boys sat in silence for a few seconds, both of them deep in thought.

At last, Glenn said, "I know it ain't goin' to be a fun conversation, but I think our best bet is for you to ask your Pa some questions about this. Try to figure out what really happened to your Ma. Don't mention us visitin' the library, just say you were wonderin' about her since he mentioned her to the sheriff. In the meantime, I'll keep tabs on what's goin' on in the town."

Levi nodded, not overly enthused about the prospect of approaching his father, but unable to come up with a better solution in the moment. "I don't think we're gonna get much outta him," he replied with a grimace.

"You're probably right. But what other choice do we have? Right now, he's our only chance we got at figurin' out what really happened on April 19th. And what that has to do with these killin's."

Chapter Five

T HE FOLLOWING DAY was Monday: market day. Usually Pa was the one who went into the market to sell the week's yield of eggs, butter, and cheese during the school year, but on this particular morning, he proposed a change of plans to the boys. "I know Sheriff Williams closed the schoolhouse to keep y'all home," he told his sons over breakfast, "but he didn't say nothin' about you goin' into town. I know you two can handle yourselves, but you need to prove to the rest of the town that we're not just gonna let them walk all over us. Gotta make a statement. Besides, I have some things to take care of. So instead of me goin' into the market and runnin' our stand, you two are gonna take my place until the schoolhouse reopens." When Austin's face lit up, Pa held up a finger. "This ain't gonna be a free for all. You can each take one day – one on Monday and one on Wednesday. Set up our normal table, barter no more than two cents off the regular sale price. If anyone gives you trouble, tell 'em to bring it up with me. Is that understood?"

"Yessir," mumbled the boys through mouthfuls of scrambled eggs.

"And if you see the sheriff, tell him to go to hell."

"Yessir," the boys repeated, a bit less enthusiastically than the first time.

As Pa sat back in his chair, Levi noticed a sallowness about his cheeks. When his father looked his way, he quickly averted his gaze. "So," said Pa. "Which of you wants to go today?"

Before Levi could even react, Austin's hand was in the air, "Me, Pa!"

Pa nodded. "Very well. Hook Samson up to the cart and I'll pack it for you. Then, you'll be on your way."

Austin stood, pumping his fist. "Yes! I'll sell everythin', Pa, promise!"

Levi opened his mouth to interject, but paused. This could be a good thing. It might give him the opportunity to talk with Pa alone and hopefully learn some new information. But almost as quickly as it arrived, the sense of good fortune dissipated. What if someone saw Austin in town that wasn't happy about it, like Jesse and Cole? What if they tried talking to him about what happened to Jed? Or tried something more aggressive than talking? The uncertainties whirled through Levi's mind, but he forced himself to close his mouth and sit back in his chair. Pa had been teaching them self-defense for a few days now. And besides, there would be plenty of people in the market. Someone would surely put a stop to any trouble that got started.

"Be smart, Aus," was all Levi said to his brother. Austin smiled in acknowledgement before running to the door to strap on his best pair of boots.

A few minutes later, Levi heard the clop of Samson's footfalls coming from outside. Through the kitchen window, he saw the mule pulling a wooden cart laden high with crates and cartons. Austin walked beside it, his face bright with a proud smile. Once Pa had seen the boy off, he reentered the house and wordlessly handed Levi a list of chores. Levi scarfed down the remainder of his breakfast and made his way outside. First on the list was milking the cows, brushing their coats, and changing their water. While it wasn't unusual for him to help Pa with the herd, he usually didn't get to spend this much time with them consecutively. He was starting to appreciate their company more as he learned each of their individual quirks and personalities.

He spent a little extra time with Piper.

Following chores were lessons, then a midday meal and free time. As Levi checked off one task after the other on his list, the impending defense lesson crept closer and closer. That would be his best opportunity to talk to Pa and he needed to make it count. He attempted to read during his few minutes of rest, but Levi couldn't stop his mind from running through scenarios of what might occur when he talked with his father. Though he managed to come up with several different ways of bringing up the topic, in his mind, the conversation always ended with his father chastising him and changing the subject.

Levi also kept forcing himself to recall the day of his mother's death and what exactly he remembered. The details of his own memory were fuzzy, but he knew the explanation his father had told him over the years by heart. He prayed that, with everything that had happened, Pa might tell the story differently this time. Provide some detail he hadn't offered before. Maybe even explain why he mentioned her to Williams.

Soon enough, Levi saw his father dragging the grain sack to the center of the field again. He steeled his breath and walked across the yard. His father explained that the lesson would cover how to maintain a proper fighting stance. Pa demonstrated how to keep low and move laterally, placing his feet shoulder-width apart. Levi followed suit. Pa gave a few recommendations and alterations, noting how the boy should lead with his left fist since he was right-handed. Even so, Levi could tell his heart wasn't in it. Pa's mind was elsewhere, as was Levi's. After a few minutes of quiet while Levi practiced, the boy cleared his throat.

"Uh, Pa?"

The old man kept his gaze on the weathered letters printed across the burlap. "Yeah?"

Levi stepped back, cracking his knuckles nervously. "With, uh, all that's been happenin', it's got me thinkin' 'bout… Ma."

Although Pa's expression never changed, Levi could've sworn he saw his eye twitch. "What about her?"

"It's just… Why'd you say her name? When you were talkin' to the sheriff about…" He trailed off, unsure of how to finish the sentence.

There was a long pause. Each second that passed made Levi's stomach twist further and further into a knot. Levi was just opening his mouth to apologize for his forwardness when Pa said, "What do you remember about what happened? To your Ma?"

Levi started, not really expecting his father to address his questions. He blinked for a moment as he determined how much to reveal. "Well – I remember Ma headin' to the woods in the afternoon. You said she went to collect berries for a pie. A few hours later, I saw you yellin' for a doctor and carryin' her into the house. You told us not to look. I ran to get the doctor and he came to see her in your study. And then…" *I never saw her again.*

Pa closed his eyes. His expression was harrowed and the boy could tell he was gathering his thoughts to speak. Levi took a step forward. He needed to catch every word of what his father said next. Any small detail could be the clue he and Glenn were searching for.

The man looked up and met his son's gaze with darkened eyes. "Your mother went to the woods that day. You're right, to collect berries. About an hour later, I heard her scream. I ran out and found her on the ground at the edge of the wood. She had… eaten the wrong berry. It was poison."

Pa's eyes flicked away and that's when Levi saw it. The hesitation, the nervous clenching of his jaw. He had told Levi and Austin that she had been poisoned by berries before and Levi had always just accepted it as fact. But his father's reaction, combined with the memory of his mother covered in blood, suddenly made him realize something wasn't right.

Pa wasn't telling the whole story.

Levi hardened his gaze, focusing on his father's face. He had found the crack in the facade. He just had to push until it broke. "If she was poisoned, why'd it look like she was… bloody?"

Pa blinked, then turned back to his son. "The berries stained her dress," he answered evenly. "I took her to my study and she died there. I buried her at night. I didn't want you two to see her like that."

Now that Levi was listening closer to his father's words, everything felt off. Like it was somehow rehearsed. He had always believed his father without a second thought. But if his memory was to be believed, his mother looked like she was covered in blood. No berry stained that shade of deep red. And the way his mother died, so unexpected and tragic – he had never heard of a plant causing that. But even if Pa was twisting the details of the story, he still didn't answer one crucial question.

"What does that have to do with Jed?"

Pa hesitated. It was slight, so slight his son almost missed it. But there was an unmistakable, hairline pause before he replied, "Two healthy people, dyin' so suddenly. Without warnin'. It ain't normal to have tragedies so close together. Town should do more about it."

Levi stared at his father. The answer was vague, without

direction. But the way his father spoke to Williams: *You know exactly what did this.* There was nothing vague about that. It was said like a fact and both men understood the meaning behind it.

And what did he mean, *the town should do more about it?* The sheriff was investigating Jed's death, so something was being done. And if Ma really died by berries, what more could they do? How could Pa connect the two? Unless… it wasn't that simple.

Why was his father lying to him?

Before he could put his thoughts together to ask another question, Pa interrupted. "Be sure to tuck your chin, protect your neck. And keep your hands in front of your face." His tone of voice commanded that the conversation was over.

Levi gritted his teeth, once again squaring up toward the burlap. His moment of opportunity had come and gone. That was probably the last time his father would be open to discussing the matter. All he knew now was although Ma's death was not what it seemed, Pa was unwilling to share any details. And he still couldn't make any sense of how it was all related to Jed's murder. After the boy continued the repetitions for another few minutes, his father finally put up a hand.

"That's enough for today," Pa said, adjusting the straw-brimmed hat atop his head. "You're skilled enough at this to handle catchin' up Austin tomorrow. I have some responsibilities to take care of. Instruct him the same way I did you. Understand?"

"Yessir."

Pa's eyes caught something over Levi's shoulder. "Looks like Aus is back. Help him tie up Samson."

Levi nodded but didn't move right away, still debating on whether he wanted to ask another question. But Pa had already turned his back and was retreating toward the house before Levi could finish making up his mind.

Just like his father said, he saw Samson, the cart, and a small figure making their way up the hill. From the person's square shoulders and gray shirt, Levi recognized him as his brother. But there was something off. A dark smear on his shirt, on his face. A limp in his step. When Levi got closer, his mouth fell open. Ausin spotted Levi and tried to hide his face, but it was too late.

"Aus, what in Christ's name happened to you?" Levi asked harshly. Austin stopped walking and dropped his head to stare at the ground. Once Levi was close enough, he put a finger under his chin and lifted his head. There were dark purple rings circling both eyes, a crimson trail leaking from his crooked nose. His shirt was laden with dirt, some patches textured and oblong in shape. Boot marks.

Austin shrugged out of Levi's hand and looked away. He couldn't meet his brother's eyes. "I fell. That's all."

"Don't start." Levi stepped back and shook his head in disdain. "It was Cole and Jesse, wasn't it?"

Austin turned to stare at him. "How'd you know that?"

"Glenn warned me yesterday they might be trouble. They've been smack talkin' us since we left school."

Austin's face contorted as he stepped toward his older brother, putting his hands out and shoving him backward. "Why the hell didn't you warn me before I left?"

Levi easily stepped back to catch himself and snapped, "Would you have listened?" Austin opened his mouth and closed it. The older brother shook his head and continued inspecting his brother's injuries. "Those bruises look pretty bad. Nose is probably broken."

Austin put a hand to his chest and winced. "Maybe some ribs, too," he muttered.

Levi gestured to him. "Didn't anyone try to stop this? Someone musta seen it, why'd they let it get this far?"

Austin swallowed, averting his gaze yet again. "They all saw it. It happened in the middle of the market." He looked up with glassy eyes, his voice tight. "They just watched, Levi. No one said or did anythin'. Most didn't even stop what they were doin'. They just *watched.*"

Levi's blood ran cold. He took a second to gather himself before grabbing Samson's lead and gently guiding him forward. "I'll take this the rest of the way. Get yourself inside and I'll help you clean up." Austin nodded and the two slowly stepped up the hill.

As they walked, Levi heard Glenn's words ring in his mind: *Imagine what they'd do when there's a motive behind the punches.* Not only were the boys brutal towards Austin in a public space, but the rest of the town didn't put a stop to it.

Which meant they condoned it.

Levi felt the hairs stand up on the back of his neck. He glanced over his shoulder toward the familiar buildings, the town he had grown up in.

It wasn't just Amos, Cole, and Jesse they had to watch out for now. It was everyone in Ainsworth.

Pa was outside when the two boys entered the house, which Levi was grateful for. The older brother grabbed a bottle of corn whiskey off the shelf and a wooden spoon from one of the cabinets. Austin shakily sat down at the head of the kitchen table; he knew what was coming. Pulling up a chair across from him, Levi sat down and handed him the bottle. "Drink," he said. Austin took a small sip and grimaced. "More." The boy gave his brother an irritated look and took a long swig. He dryly coughed and shuddered before placing it on the table. Satisfied, Levi held out the spoon.

"What's that for?" asked Austin.

"Bite down on it."

Austin made another face, but obliged and closed his eyes. Levi noticed his hands clenched in his lap, but it didn't stop them from shaking. The older brother leaned forward, gently placing his fingers on either side of Austin's nose. Even at the light touch, he felt the boy tense.

"Alright," muttered Levi. "On the count of three. One—"

With a sharp twist of his hands, Levi snapped the cartilage back into place. The wooden spoon crackled as Austin clenched down. To his credit, the only sound he made was a soft whimper. Levi sat back to examine his work. Although swollen, his brother's nose appeared to be straight again. A dark trail of blood leaked from one nostril.

"Should be good now," Levi sighed, exhaling softly. It was only then that Austin opened his eyes and removed the spoon from his mouth. His teeth had left indentations on the handle.

Austin slowly raised a hand to touch his nose. "How'd you learn to do that?"

Levi shrugged. "Glenn had a habit of pokin' at kids bigger than him when we were 'round your age. He's wisened up a bit nowadays. But I have plenty of experience with fixin' him up after a scuffle. I even put his finger back in place, once. You're not the only one who likes to get into fights. "

"I don't *like* gettin' into fights," his brother snapped.

"Whatever." Levi gestured to the boy's bloody face and matted hair. "Get yourself washed up for supper."

Austin started to turn away, but paused and looked back. "You won't say anythin' about this to Pa, will you?"

Levi shrugged. "I won't. But you probably won't be able to hide it from him."

Austin glowered at his brother and stomped upstairs.

Food was ready and on the table a short while later. Pa came in from the barn, smelling like sweat and the outdoors. He filled his plate and sat down at the head of the table. Levi and Austin made their plates and sat as well, although Austin kept his head down. Once they were all seated at the table, Levi saw Pa glance at the youngest brother.

The man narrowed his eyes. "Lookit me, boy."

Austin hesitated before raising his head to meet his father's gaze. As Pa scanned his face, the blood rushed to the boy's cheeks. The man clenched his jaw. "Levi," he muttered, gaze still glued to Austin. "You willin' to run the stall both days?"

Levi sat up slightly in his chair. "Yessir."

Pa gave one more hard look at the boy, then shifted his attention back to his meal. The rest of supper was spent in silence. Levi glanced over at Austin every few minutes. The boy barely ate, only nudged his food with his fork.

Once their plates were cleared, Austin hurried upstairs and slammed his bedroom door behind him. Pa went into his study a few minutes later. Neither of them showed their faces for the rest of the night. Levi took charge of the late-night tasks, sweeping the kitchen floor and washing the remaining dishes. When he ensured every lantern was darkened, he retreated to his own room for the night. The house was eerily quiet while he changed into his evening attire, lit an oil lamp, and sat in bed. A choir of crickets serenaded outside his window, lulling him into a sense of calm as he read the story of Beowolf. Only when he felt the book slipping inadvertently from his hands did he snuff out the lamp and lay down for the night.

To Levi, it felt like a blink. But when he next opened his eyes, he found it was dark outside. The darkness filling the room told him it was not yet morning. He rolled over in bed and closed his eyes, willing himself to return to sleep before he became fully conscious.

A strange feeling washed over him. Like the air was filled with electricity, racing through his veins and forcing his hair on end. The sensation was becoming more familiar to him, less unnatural every time it came about. First at the forest, then the night Jed was killed – and now.

Levi's gaze was drawn to the bedroom window. Like there was something beyond the pane of glass, silently calling out to be seen. He stood as if in a trance. His feet seemed to move of their own accord, walking to stand before the window. It revealed the side of the farm, close to the edge of the fence where the chicken coop stood. The field was washed in a soft white light, courtesy of the full moon.

But Levi wasn't focused on the moon. He was staring at the figure standing in the middle of the grass.

It was impossible to make out any distinguishing features of the person in the darkness, but it was definitely a human outline. Standing on two legs, two long arms hanging by their sides. They were facing the house, positioned a few feet from the side of the chicken coop. Levi could just make out the glint of eyes sitting in its head. He couldn't tell where the figure was looking, but for some reason, he felt it was staring directly at him. He stood there, not daring to move a muscle. His mind raced as to who it could be and why they were there in the dead of night. Was it Glenn, here to visit him? Amos, ready to exact his revenge? Or whatever murdered Jed? But something about the way the thing was standing, it was so – unnerving. Levi couldn't take his eyes off it. No human stood that still. And who knew how long they'd been there before Levi noticed.

There was something hanging around its waist. It looked almost like a thick skirt, interwoven pieces that swayed ever so slightly in the breeze.

The two stayed locked in that position for what felt like hours, but Levi knew was only minutes. Even though the boy wasn't moving, his heart raced like he was running. A bead of sweat traced down his forehead, trickling into his eye. It burned and he instinctively wiped at it.

Just when he reopened his eyes, there was movement near the barn. Levi swiveled his head toward it, and saw it was one of the herd sticking its head out of a side window.

His gaze was only away from it for a moment, and–

It was gone.

Levi stepped forward, pressing both palms against the window. He scanned the dimly lit yard, searching for any sign of it. A bird flew across the sky, but aside from that, the night was calm.

As quickly as the strange feeling had come, it had gone. Whatever it was that had caused it was no longer nearby. But Levi's heart took much longer to slow its desperate pounding.

He stood there for several long minutes barely daring to blink. Then, his feet slowly stepped him backward toward his cot. With shaking hands, he laid down and pulled the sheet over him.

The boy's eyes remained open the rest of the night.

Chapter Six

WHEN LEVI APPROACHED the kitchen table the following morning, he and Austin stared at each other; Levi inspected Austin's darkened bruises and scabbed cuts while Austin took in Levi's bloodshot eyes underlined with deep bags.

"You doin' alright?" Austin asked his brother.

"Yeah," Levi replied, slumping into the chair across from him. "Just didn't sleep well."

Their father was seated on the other side of the table, an empty place setting in front of him. If Levi appeared as if he hadn't slept for a night, Pa looked like he hadn't rested in weeks. His face was lined with wrinkles, his eyes glazed and red-rimmed. He was wearing yesterday's clothes – though the more Levi thought about it, it might've been the same clothes he wore two days ago.

Suddenly, the man stood. He dazedly walked to the counter and grabbed a piece of bread, then attempted to pour himself a cup of coffee. He spilled over the edges of the mug, the pot shaking in his hand. After staring at the mess for a moment, he placed the coffee pot back down and nodded to the boys. Pa slowly made his way back up the stairs, shoving the slice of bread in his mouth as he did so.

"Looks like he didn't have a good night, either," muttered Austin, reaching over to get the dishrag lying on the table. He walked to the other side of the kitchen, carefully mopping up the excess of his father's beverage. "You think he's ill or somethin'?"

Levi didn't answer, instead twirling his fork in his hand while his mind worked. "Did Pa give us a list of chores for today?" he asked softly.

Austin shrugged. "Don't think so."

His older brother glanced outside. "We know what needs to be done. Let's take care of the animals. We'll talk during self-defense lessons."

"But… you think Pa's gonna do lessons today?"

"He told me to catch you up on what I learned yesterday."

"Alright. What'll I do for chores?"

Levi assigned Austin to cleaning out the chicken coop and collecting the day's yield of eggs. When he was done, he was to come over to the barnhouse and help Levi finish milking and feeding the cattle.

The boys hustled off to their stations, in a hurry to take their mind off the situation at hand. Austin didn't have much trouble distracting himself and Levi heard him humming a song under his breath as he worked. The older brother grabbed the nearest pail and tried to get into the rhythm of milking, but found his eyes kept wandering toward the spot near the chicken coop where the figure had been standing the previous evening.

The more he thought about it, the less sure he was that he had seen what he thought he'd seen. While he had definitely seen someone, a voice in the back of his mind kept telling him something wasn't right about it all. Not that seeing a person on the farm in the middle of the night was normal, but he couldn't ignore the chill that accompanied seeing the figure. And the way it stood impossibly still.

He had probably just been dreaming, he decided. Or stuck in that half-dream half-awake state where your mind can play tricks on you. There was no reason for someone to be on the property at that time of night, or any way for them to possibly disappear as quickly as they did.

Unless the figure had something to do with whatever was going on in town. But Levi didn't want to consider that possibility.

"Need help?" Levi jumped to his feet, spinning around to stare at his brother. Austin took a step back, eyebrows raised. "Sorry, didn't mean to startle you. I just finished with the coop."

"You didn't startle me." Levi took a breath to calm his now racing heart, then sat back down on the stool. "This is the last one that needs milkin'. Start changin' out the hay and gettin' more feed, wouldja?"

"Alright."

A few minutes later, both brothers finished their respective tasks and went inside to start on their schoolwork. Levi was miles ahead of the class in his lessons by now, but he didn't mind. It only meant he'd have less work to do when he got back. Austin seemed less enthused with keeping up with his classmates and let out several aggravated sighs as he worked.

Lunch followed their lessons, and Levi put together a meal for the pair. While they ate, the two looked to the stairway every few minutes.

Their father never joined them.

Once the boys had cleared their plates, it was time. Levi walked Austin over to the grain sacks. He briefly explained the main points of what Pa had taught him the previous day and demonstrated the proper footwork and a few punches. Austin watched intently before replicating. Levi made some minor corrections, reminding him to keep his fists up and his feet shoulder-width apart. The younger brother quickly got the hang of it and Levi had him do some more repetitions as Pa had requested he do the previous day. When Austin had found a rhythm with it, Levi took a breath.

"I have somethin' to tell you."

Austin paused, glancing towards his brother. "What about?"

"About what really happened to Ma."

The boy dropped his hands, fully staring at his brother. "What do ya mean?"

Levi gestured toward the grain sack. Only when Austin begrudgingly began his repetitions again did Levi drop his voice to a whisper and say, "After Pa mentioned Ma's name to Williams, I got to wonderin' if there was somethin' we were missin', or Pa didn't tell us. So, Glenn and I did some diggin'. 'Least, we tried to. You probably don't remember, but when Ma passed, there was an article written about it in the paper." Austin nodded his understanding, but his slightly blank expression told Levi this was new information. "Well, when Glenn and I went lookin' for it in the library archives, it was missin'."

"Why was it missin'?"

"Dunno. Maybe someone misplaced it… or someone could be tryin' to hide somethin'." Austin turned away, clearly mulling over this new advancement, but Levi wasn't finished. "There's more. Yesterday while you were at the market, I asked Pa about what exactly happened to Ma the night she died. He told me the same story he always did, about the berries in the woods killin' her… but somethin' was wrong. I think he's lyin' to us."

Austin's brows furrowed. "You do?"

"I do." Levi closed his eyes and replayed the memory in his mind. "The night it happened, I remember Pa comin' into the house, carryin' Ma. She was covered in blood. But Pa said it was poisonin' that killed her, from berries. At first, I thought I was just rememberin' the day wrong. After talkin' with him, though, I think Pa might be hidin' the truth. He was actin' jumpy and his story wasn't addin' up."

"But Pa never lies to us."

"I know. That's why I'm thinkin' Williams has got somethin' to do with it."

Austin stared at his brother strangely. "How so?"

Levi glanced around the property, making sure they were still alone. To his best knowledge, they were, so he added, "Pa ain't one to bite his tongue. And once Williams left on Friday, he sure was quiet 'bout this whole thing. I think Williams said somethin' to him."

"Like what?"

"Somethin' to keep him quiet. Somethin' bad enough to make Pa not fight him on keepin' us home from school, too. But I'm pretty sure Pa knows somethin' about Ma that Williams don't want the rest of the town to know. Includin' the two of us."

Austin landed a few more hits on the sack before replying, "So what you're sayin' is Pa's scared of somethin'."

"Exactly. I think Pa wants to figure out exactly what's goin' on, but Williams won't let him for whatever reason." Levi paused to glance toward the house. "And Pa don't seem to be in his right mind."

His younger brother frowned. "Whaddya mean by that?"

"I mean him shuttin' himself in his study for hours on end."

"He said he's workin' on somethin'."

"If he's workin' on anythin', it should be his farm." Levi shook his head. "I dunno what he's doin' up there, but all I know is he ain't actin' like he should be. Which means fixin' this is up to us."

"What're we gonna do about anythin'? All of Ainsworth already thinks we're hidin' somethin', if they see us actin' strange they're just gonna think we did it even more."

Levi leaned in. "Do you have any money saved up?"

The younger brother thought for a moment. "Maybe half a dollar. Why?"

"We gotta buy ourselves a weapon. Somethin' of our own that we can use to hunt this killer down."

"Like a gun?"

"Exactly like a gun."

"Why don't we use one of Pa's?"

"If we stole a gun and Pa caught us, he would kill us faster than any bear could." Levi sighed and murmured, "We gotta get out of this on our own. And that means findin' whatever killed Jed and killin' it ourselves. We can bring it to the sheriff. Then they'll know for sure it wasn't us that caused this and we can clear our names once and for all."

"You really think we can kill a bear by ourselves?"

Levi started to answer, but paused. Did a bear really kill Jed? It was definitely an animal that killed Caroline and Ryder, and he only saw the strange figure for the first time last night. But was it possible that person could've been Jed's murderer? If nothing else, it was the first evidence he had seen of something unusual on the farm aside from the tracks. "I'm not sure it's a bear we're lookin' for."

Austin cocked his head to one side. "Why do you say that? We saw those tracks."

"I know – I think a bear killed Caroline. But maybe not Jed." The boy paused as the reminder of the previous night's chill washed over him. "I saw a person outside the farm last night. He was standin' near the chicken coop, watchin' me."

Austin's eyes bulged wide and he swiveled his head toward the coop on the other side of the property. "You did? What'd he look like?"

"I couldn't really see him, it was too dark." Austin gave him a look, and Levi hurried on, "But it was definitely a person. I saw the outline and all. Somethin' was off, though. He was standin' still, still like I ain't never seen a person stand. And while I was starin' at him, I looked away for no more than a half a second and then – he was gone. Just like that."

The younger brother turned back to the burlap sack. "You sure it wasn't a dream?"

"I swear on Ma's life."

Austin squared up toward the grain, but kept his fists frozen in front of him. "If you couldn't see what he looked like," he said slowly, "that means it coulda been anyone."

"I know." Levi put a hand on his brother's shoulder. "The only people we can trust are each other. So I need to know you're on my side here."

His brother glanced toward Levi's hand and back up to his face. "You don't think we can trust Pa?"

Levi hesitated, then relented, "If he's lyin' to us about Ma, who knows what else he ain't bein' entirely truthful about." Austin's face fell, but he nodded his understanding. Levi went on, "Save up whatever money you can and I'll do the same. We need a way to protect ourselves – and a way to kill whoever it is when we cross paths with him again."

"How're we gonna get all that money?"

Levi had a plan, but he wasn't ready to share it with his brother quite yet. "We'll find a way. In the meantime, keep an eye out for anythin' suspicious. But don't go outside the farm by yourself, especially at night. You understand?"

"Yeah."

"Good. Now, switch to the other side and finish up for the day."

Austin paused just a second more before altering his feet and shifting his fists. He took a breath and began again.

With the crunch of grain filling his ears, Levi felt a tingling at the nape of his neck. The cool breeze that swept across the field set his teeth on edge.

Someone was watching them.

Levi kept his expression neutral so as to not distract his brother and scanned the surrounding field for the source of his unease. The herd was alone in the pasture, the flock locked in the coop. His gaze eventually stopped on the topmost window of the house, facing the yard.

The shadowy silhouette of their father stood at the window, watching the boys work from above.

Levi tipped his hat to the man and forced his attention back on his brother. If he was honest with himself, he didn't feel right keeping something like this from Pa. But if this morning was any indication of his father's mental state, it was evident Pa was not thinking clearly right now. Like Levi said, the only people Austin and himself could trust were each other.

The following day was Wednesday, the second market day of the week. Once Austin and Levi were seated at the kitchen table eating breakfast, the boys were surprised to hear the thump of their father's footsteps on the staircase. He passed the pair without a word and exited through the front door. The brothers were quiet while they watched him walk to the shed and withdraw something from inside. As the man crossed the field, Levi spotted the glint of the shears clutched in his right hand. The boys exchanged looks and returned to their food. Every few days, their father visited their mother's grave to tend to the surrounding weeds and plants. He likely wouldn't be back for some time.

After finishing his food, Levi went outside. Austin followed, but remained silent as Levi began stacking the blocks of cheese and wooden buckets of eggs into Samson's cart. Almost nothing was sold on Monday due to the skirmish and there was already plenty more stock that needed to be sold as well if they were to stay on track. Levi had his work cut out for him.

As Levi was pulling on his jacket, he turned to Austin. The young boy had his arms crossed in front of him, lips pressed tightly together. The despondent look on his face tugged at his brother's heartstrings. "Hey," said Levi. "Keep an eye on Pa, will ya? Make sure to get him some grub when he comes back inside."

Austin nodded, eyes fixed on his boots. "Alright."

Levi smiled apologetically and walked to where Samson stood at the back of the barn. He carefully untethered him and tied him to the front of the cart. Luckily, when they had the most to sell, they were headed downhill into town and the weight would work in Samson's favor. He hoped the mule would have much less to carry when they had to make the trek back uphill later that evening.

Ainsworth had a small market square near the town center that bustled with buyers and sellers every weekday. There weren't many stalls, so most vendors rotated out one or two days of the week. The Oakley's stall days were Monday and Wednesday. Levi and Austin didn't visit the market during the school year, but during the summer they were always there, unless there was more important work to be done on the farm. Since Pa was one of the sellers that had frequented the market the longest, he had one of the better stall locations: a long table with a canopy overhead close to the entrance.

As Levi and Samson lumbered toward the stall, he saw some owners throw looks at him. Nothing overly intrusive, but enough for the boy to notice. He saw a few of them turn to exchange whispers, then stare back at the boy. Some of them seemed curious. Some pitiful. Some disdainful.

Just get through the day, Levi thought to himself, keeping his eyes on the dirt road in front of him. *Just make it through one day and they'll leave you alone.*

After tying Samson to a side post, the boy quietly laid out the cheese and butter on the table. He carefully lined up the buckets of eggs and setup two signs, one detailing the prices and another listing the available products. Glancing around, he noted some familiar faces selling knitted baskets, bread, and jarred preserves. A woman he didn't recognize was selling candles. Levi politely smiled at those that caught his eye, but they quickly glanced away and pretended they hadn't seen.

Just one day.

A few minutes later, people began filing in. Although the stall owners appeared wary of his presence in the market, the shoppers didn't seem to have the same issue. A few of their expressions soured when they spotted him, but most bought their weekly supply of eggs and butter without question.

The hours passed and around noon, Levi took out a biscuit layered with cheese and ham from his rucksack. At that point, he had sold about half of his supply – not bad, but still had a bit more to do if he was to make up for the poor performance on Monday. He might need to lower the prices if he wanted to do better in the afternoon.

He was preparing to take his first bite when he saw them.

They attempted to remain cloaked in shadows, flitting between the cover of canopies. Even with the light never touching their faces, Levi knew from their outlines who the pair was.

Jesse and Cole.

Levi ducked his head down and turned toward the booth, heart pounding in his chest. He suspected they'd return at some point, but not so soon, not after what happened to Austin on Monday. They must have asked around to figure out which days Levi and his family held a table at the market. With trembling hands, he feigned rearranging the products displayed on the table in front of him. He needed to craft his next move very carefully.

Levi was pretty sure they weren't interested in a conversation and he certainly didn't want to cause another scene. The rest of the town still clearly carried resentment from the incident earlier in the week – another would only increase the tension further. Besides, if Austin was telling the truth, then he was on his own with this fight and no one was coming to help him if things went sour. *They just watched.*

Glancing up, Levi's blood ran cold as he saw they were only three stalls away. He knew this was his chance to make the first move. Before the situation got out of hand, he needed to explain his side and at least make an attempt to deescalate. He took a breath, squared his shoulders, and stared directly at the loitering figures: "Jesse and Cole."

After the pair glanced at each other and seemed to exchange silent words, they emerged to stand in front of Levi's table. Levi stepped in front of the table, shoving his shoulders back. "Whaddya want?" he called.

Cole glowered and spat at his feet. "You ain't welcome here."

"And why's that?"

Jesse gave him a strange look. "'Cause you and Austin were the ones who killed Jed."

Apparently, Glenn had been right about their classmates jumping to conclusions. "My brother and I had nothin' to do with what happened to Jed." Levi held up his hands. "Swear to God, we weren't even near him that night. The sheriff said we're suspects, not that we're guilty."

"The *only* suspects," Jesse replied with a sneer. "And we know what Austin said to Jed and Amos. Y'all were meetin' that night to fight. Stop lyin' and fess up to what you done."

Levi shook his head, letting his hands fall to his sides and dropping his voice to a low whisper. "You honestly think Austin and I coulda ripped a boy apart like that?" He stepped forward. "There's somethin' else goin' on here. I had one of my herd killed, and Glenn lost his pup. All within the span of a few days. You don't think that's strange?"

For a moment, Levi saw a sliver of doubt cross Cole's face. But just as quickly as it appeared, it vanished, concealed in a burning rage. "Stop tryin' to change the subject," he grunted. Before Levi could react, Cole strode forward and shoved both hands into the boy's chest. Levi stumbled backwards into the table and toppled over one of the baskets. Several eggs cascaded down, spraying the ground with white shell and yellow yolk. He heard Samson stamp and snort behind him, irritated by the sudden commotion.

The sound of Jesse and Cole's chuckles filled Levi's ears as he straightened. His father's words rang in his mind. *Feet shoulder-width apart. Form the fists, thumbs wrapped over your pointer and middle fingers. Head high, don't hunch.*

Make sure your hit lands on the knuckles.

Once the pair saw the look on Levi's face, their mirth instantly dissipated. They raised their fists in unison and narrowed their eyes at the boy. After a pause where it seemed like the whole market held its breath, Levi stepped forward and swung.

Cole deftly avoided the blow with a quick turn, then launched a return aimed at Levi's middle. The boy saw the punch coming and twisted out of its path. He felt Cole's knuckles graze the side of his shirt. Just when he regained his footing, a boot landed a kick to the back of his knees, sending him sprawling to the ground. He flipped over to find himself staring into Jesse's snarling smile.

Levi had no chance to respond as the boy leapt on top of him and grabbed his shirt with both hands. He seized Jesse's forearms and shoved his elbows into the boy's chest, buying him room to breathe. Cole's voice taunted from somewhere above and behind him. Even while the boys wrestled, Levi's mind remained clear. He thought of his father and tried to imagine what he'd say in a situation like this. *You're outnumbered, boy. It ain't a fair fight. So don't play fair.*

Levi's eyes snapped open and his head swiveled to both sides, searching. *There.*

The boy gritted his teeth and swiftly released one of his hands from Jesse, reaching to his left. He curled his fingers around the mess of yolky egg shells and dust. In one swift motion, he jammed his hand into Jesse's face, pressing and twisting the mix-ture into his eyes. Though he winced when the fragmented shells bit into his hand, he only pressed harder as he felt Jesse's grip on him loosen.

Jesse fell back and grabbed at his face, giving Levi the oppor-tunity he was looking for. He sat upright, shoving Jesse down and following him to the ground. Now on top, he began landing hit after hit, one after the other. Again, his father spoke in his mind. He pictured a grain sack in front of him. *Left. Right. Left. Right.*

As the blows rained down, the blood from Levi's split

knuckles mixed with that of the boy beneath him. For a fraction of a second, Levi saw his brother's bruised and broken face flash in his mind. He drew his fist back and hurled one final blow at Jesse's nose.

He felt a bony crunch.

Levi released the boy and sat back, chest heaving with every breath. Jesse rolled to his side, curling in on himself and covering his bloodied face with both hands. When Levi held up his shaking fists, he stared at the rivelet of red tracing a path down his knuckles. Everything grew quiet now and the pounding of adrenaline slowly dissipated from his ears.

That's when Levi felt a hand wrap itself around the hair on the back of his head.

Levi's head snapped upward and a searing pain raced over his scalp as Cole dragged him to the ground. Suddenly, the boy was on top of him. Levi only got a glimpse of the fury filling his opponent's eyes before the first blow landed. Pain blossomed from his cheekbone as his head was thrown to the right. Another hit came and Levi instantly tasted metal. He grit his teeth and shut his eyes, waiting for the next punch.

But it never came.

He heard a scuffle and the weight was lifted off his chest. Levi sat up painfully, blinking sweat and blood out of his eyes. There was another figure in the fray now, with dusty blonde hair and a lopsided smile he'd recognize anywhere.

"Glenn," Levi breathed with a grin.

His friend glanced at him. "I told you I'd have your back," he chuckled and turned his attention back to Cole. Cole seemed frazzled now, his form less refined and his shoulders hunched. His eyes flicked from Glenn to Levi and then to Jesse. He hesitated for a moment and dropped his hands.

"Let's get the hell outta here," Cole grunted, snapping his fingers at Jesse. Without a word, the boy picked himself up off the ground and scampered over. The pair gave one last leering look at Levi and Glenn, Jesse through squinted and swollen eyes, before sprinting back in the direction from which they came.

The remaining pair glanced around in the sudden quiet. Levi realized the entire market had stopped what they were doing to watch them. His face instantly grew warm, but his friend stepped forward.

Glenn waved his arms in the air. "Alright, nothin' to see here. As you were."

A murmuring settled over the square as people resumed their activities. Levi caught the eye of the lady selling candles, who gave him a sly smile of approval. He nodded in return. Maybe not quite everyone in town was against him.

It was only when the boys were out of sight that Levi breathed a sigh of relief and embraced his friend. "Thanks," he said, releasing him and grinning from ear to ear. "You really saved my ass right there."

Glenn shrugged, but Levi saw in his expression how much his words meant to him. "I know. You're welcome." He glanced over his shoulder in the direction the boys had left. "Hopefully that keeps them outta your hair for a bit. They won't start a fight unless they have the upperhand, that's for sure. I was nervous Amos was gonna show up and join in, but I guess he's still stuck at home."

Levi dabbed at his lip with his finger. It came away stained red. "How did you know to get here?"

"I heard about Jesse and Cole roughin' up your brother on Monday, and figured they might come back the second day. So I kept my eye on the street while I worked in the field and came over once I saw them headed into town." His face darkened as he changed subjects. "You get a chance to talk to your Pa?"

"Yeah," Levi replied, brushing dust off his sleeves. "Didn't really learn anythin' new. Still gave the same story about the poisoned berries – but I'm almost positive he's lyin', now. Somethin' about the way he said it just didn't seem right."

"And he didn't mention nothin' about his arrest?"

"I only got far enough to ask about Ma before he shut me down."

His friend shook his head, saying, "Damn. I was really hopin' we'd get somethin' useful outta him. We'll just have to look for somethin' else." Glenn glanced up at the clock tower in the center square. "I ought to be gettin' back. My Pa'll be lookin' for me."

Just as Glenn was turning away, Levi stopped him with, "Before you go, I got a question."

"Shoot."

Levi hesitated. "You didn't happen to come by my farm last night, did you? A little after midnight?"

His friend gave him a look. "No. Why, did you see somethin'?"

Levi shook his head, his friend's response only deepening the pit in his stomach. "No, I just – thought I saw somethin'. Probably just a dream." He didn't have the time or energy to explain right now. Besides, the more he thought about it, maybe it was a dream. That seemed like the easier explanation.

"Alright, well… lemme know if you see anythin' else."

"I will." Levi forced a smile on his face. "Now, get back to your farm. And thank you, again. You're a good man." Glenn nodded in return and took off.

Levi used the next few minutes to pull himself together and tend to the worst of his wounds. He ended up getting off pretty lucky, only a split lip and a gnarly bruise on one cheek. It could've ended up much worse. He really owed it to Glenn.

It might've been because of the newly acquired injuries, but Levi ended up selling much better in the afternoon than he did in the morning. By the time the sun began to set and the rest of the sellers were packing up, he only had half a dozen eggs remaining and a few blocks of cheese. He counted his money carefully, then slipped about a fifth of the profits into his boot. If his father asked, he would just say most people bartered down. Hopefully, it wasn't enough to garner suspicion from his old man.

The cart was noticeably lighter than it was that morning and Samson trotted happily uphill on the way back home. Once the pair arrived, Levi returned the mule to the barn, gathered the remaining supplies and stepped through the front door.

Pa and Austin were already seated at the kitchen table when the boy entered. They looked up expectantly from their bowls of stew. "How'd it go?" Pa asked cautiously. At a quick glance, he already seemed to be in a better state than the day prior. But his eyes still looked slightly hollowed, his skin a shade too pale. Levi was thankful for the improvement, though, no matter how small.

"Sold all but half a dozen eggs and three blocks," Levi replied, shutting the door behind him and starting to unlace his boots.

It was quiet for a moment. "And how do the others look?" asked Pa knowingly.

Levi paused, slowly raising his gaze to meet his father's. "Worse."

For the first time in days, Pa smiled.

Chapter Seven

"You swear you broke his nose? Like, really broke it?"

This was the third time Austin had asked Levi to regale him with the story of the market altercation and every time he had made sure to emphasize that point. His older brother had given up working on his own schoolwork that morning, but he was secretly happy to detail his and Glenn's victory over and over again.

"Yep. Felt it give way and everythin'. Unless someone sets it proper like I did for you, he's gonna be lookin' real lopsided for the rest of his days."

Austin sat backwards in his chair, a gleeful smile spreading over his face. "With them out of the way, now we can put all our energy into solvin' Jed's murder," he said. "Work on catchin' the real criminal."

"Before we do any investigatin'," Levi interrupted, "we gotta put some work into protectin' our farm."

"Why do we gotta do that? Whoever killed Jed is more dangerous than a bear."

Levi paused, struggling to put his intuition into words. "Maybe so, but I still wanna add some stones to the base of the fences to make sure none of the others get torn out, by a bear or anythin' else. And I think we should get a new padlock for the barn door."

"Did Pa ask you to do all that?"

"No," Levi admitted. "But just 'cause there might be a murderer around don't mean we can forget about losin' Caroline and Ryder."

After pondering it, Austin nodded his reluctant agreement. "When're we gonna go back to the woods? We're not gonna find any more clues stayin' on the farm."

"Once we're sure the farm is safe, we can keep searchin'," Levi assured him and glanced toward the study above him. "And keep your voice down about the whole woods thing. Pa wouldn't be too pleased if he heard we were plannin' on sneakin' out again."

"Alright. But like you said, we gotta do somethin'. And Pa's no help."

"We *are* gonna do somethin'. Once we're sure the farm is safe." Levi drew absent-mindedly on his slate as he spoke. "I guess Pa's done givin' us work in the meantime. Maybe he thinks we know everythin' by now."

"I don't mind. Means we get to do what we want."

"Uh huh." When Levi glanced up to see Austin staring off into the distance, he snapped, "Hey. Finish your assignment, then I'm gonna head outside and teach you another self-defense lesson."

Austin cocked his head to one side. "Pa taught you another lesson?"

"No. But imma teach you a move that Glenn showed me: it's called a chokehold."

The younger brother grinned maliciously. "I like the sound of that."

"Then finish your work."

With only minimal complaining on Austin's part, the boys completed the rest of their assignments and continued with their normal schedule throughout the day. Levi did end up teaching Austin the chokehold, and how to position yourself to gain an advantage over your opponent. Austin was apprehensive at first, but was becoming more confident in his abilities.

A few minutes into the lesson, something caught Levi's eye moving along the edge of the fence. This time, he didn't have to think twice as to who it might be. He told Austin to review some of the old moves they practiced earlier that week before jogging around the opposite side of the barn, closest to where Glenn was creeping his way onto the farm. While he approached, Levi spotted something clutched in his left hand. It looked like a paper of some sort.

"Back so soon?" Levi called, making a final sprint toward the side of the barn. But Levi's smile died on his lips as soon as he saw his friend's solemn expression. "Glenn, what happened?"

The boy said nothing, instead spreading open the paper in his hand. Not just paper, Levi realized. Newspaper. Across the top of the page read, *Horses Massacred During the Night.* And there, in the middle of the page, were his and his brother's names:

Brothers Levi and Austin Oakley are currently the only suspects in the murder of Jed Lawson, which occurred much in the same fashion as these recent killings. Levi couldn't read the whole article from where he was standing, but he was able to make out the words "jail," "trial," and "hanging" toward the end of the article.

"You can't be serious," Levi whispered.

Glenn snapped the newspaper shut and tossed it to him. "I wish I was jokin'." As Levi skimmed the page, he continued, "They're really not gonna let this go. They're not even bein' subtle now – they're just outright blamin' the two of you for anythin' that goes wrong in town."

"The sheriff is sayin' this?"

"He apparently told the paper about what happened to Jed and the fact that you two are under suspicion. It's the writer who's makin' it out to seem that the two of you are guilty, not just suspects. Although I wouldn't be surprised if he was encouraged in that direction."

"Entire horses torn apart," Levi read aloud. "Who do they think we are? Some sorta maniacs goin' around, sneakin' onto other people's farms and dismantlin' their livestock in our free time?"

Glenn shrugged and replied, "Listen, it ain't me you need to convince. You gotta talk to the sheriff and get him off your case. He's the only one the town'll listen to. I'm afraid if we don't convince them soon, stuff is gonna happen. Worse than what happened in the market."

Levi crumbled up the newspaper and tossed it into one of the feeding troughs behind him. "Is there anyone in Ainsworth that don't believe it's us?"

"I mean, there's a few real religious folks paintin' crosses on their doors, thinkin' the Devil might be behind it. But most of the town is suspicious of you two."

"And the sheriff hasn't said anythin' about other suspects?"

"None that I've heard of."

Levi chewed on his lip for a moment, mind whirring. "I guess I can see Williams tomorrow morning, try to talk some sense into him." Another thought hit him. "In fact, Williams might have some more information about Ma. That's worth askin' about."

Glenn's eyes brightened. "Yeah, you're right. How're you gonna sneak off the farm?"

"I'll just head out tomorrow mornin'. If Pa asks, I'll just say

I'm headed to the market to grab food for dinner. Bread and such, things we can't make ourselves. But he hasn't come out of his room in a few days, so I doubt he'll ask."

Glenn frowned. "A few days?"

Levi brushed aside the question, not wanting to divulge his father's true state. "Yeah. But Williams seemed to know what Pa was talkin' about when he was makin' those strange remarks about Jed and Ma. So if Pa won't tell me, maybe Williams will."

In the back of his mind, he realized he might also have some leverage to use on the sheriff as well. Williams didn't know about the mysterious figure Levi saw in the night, so that information might be useful to him. Hopefully the man wouldn't question whether or not it was a dream.

His friend nodded. "You save up enough for a gun yet?"

"Not yet. Snagged some extra cash from the sales yesterday, though. Until then, keep doin' what you're doin', and let me know if you hear anything' strange. 'Specially from anyone who's had somethin' killed on their property."

"You got it."

The two boys stared in the direction of the town for a moment, each trapped in their own thoughts. "Alright," Levi eventually said. "You best get back home."

"Yeah," Glenn replied and tipped his hat to his friend. "Stay safe."

"Thanks, Glenn." Once he saw his friend creeping back toward town, Levi ducked around the corner of the barn back toward the grain sacks.

As soon as he was within earshot, Austin shouted, "What happened?" Levi gave him a look, and Austin glanced toward their father's window. Lucky for him, it appeared like their father wasn't watching.

Levi stepped up to his brother and said, "Nothin'. Glenn just wanted to check in with me after the fight yesterday. Now, let me see what you've been practicin'." Austin clearly wasn't convinced, but didn't press the matter.

Although Pa seemed a bit more lucid than the previous day, tonight was yet another night where he didn't show for supper. Once the last of the pink had dissipated from the sky and Austin began yawning, Levi glanced one final time at the staircase. It was empty. He silently stood, grabbed a plate from the cupboard and spooned a portion onto it. The boy crept up the stairs and stepped toward his father's closed study door. He carefully placed the full plate, knife, and fork beside it, and knocked twice.

There was no reply.

He waited a second longer before returning downstairs to finish cleaning up for the night. By the time he made his way to his room a half hour later, the plate and utensils were gone. Levi gave a small smile, then headed into his own room and shut the door.

The next morning, Levi and Austin went about their usual routine. While even a week ago it would've been unheard of for Pa to skip a meal with his sons, it was now becoming commonplace. After they finished their basic farm duties, Levi explained to Austin his tasks on improving the farm's defenses. They hauled the largest rocks they could find around the property and placed them at varying points around the fence. Levi demonstrated to Austin the proper way to stack them to reinforce the posts and provide the most support.

"Why do I gotta do all the borin' stuff?" huffed Austin, pulling on a pair of work gloves. "I wanna go into town."

"That didn't go so well last time."

"But I've learned how to fight properly! I'm ready!"

"Maybe you can try again next week," Levi responded, clearly trying to delay the issue. "Remember, if Pa asks where I am, I'm pickin' up more bread and fruit. Got it?"

"Yeah, whatever."

Once Levi was convinced Austin wouldn't totally abandon his work as soon as he left, he went back inside the house and grabbed his father's portion of the money from the market sales on Wednesday. Unsurprisingly, it hadn't been touched. He also pulled his rucksack off the hanger and took the widest brim hat his father owned. It wasn't the best disguise, and the hat was a tad too big for Levi's head. But it covered most of his face when he was looking down, which he hoped would be enough to deter unwanted stares.

Even though he had the perfect alibi in place, Levi's stomach still fluttered with nervousness as he walked down the path into town. He was sure any minute his father would run out of the house, scream at him for disobeying and drag him by the ear back inside. But either his father didn't see him or his father didn't care, for the walk into town was peaceful aside from Levi's inner anxiety.

First, he stopped at the market to bring some legitimacy to his fib. He bought some apples from one vendor, a few jarred goods from another. But when he tried to purchase a loaf of bread, the shop owner started acting strange.

"How much for that one?" Levi asked, pointing to a golden-brown loaf to the right of the table.

The woman running the booth continued rearranging the bread as if she hadn't heard him. Her gaze seemed pointedly fixed at the table in front of her.

The boy hesitated, then waved a hand in front of the woman. "Hello? Can you hear me?"

Ever so subtly, the woman broke her concentration and her eyes flicked to Levi. But immediately after, she turned away and began counting her money at the back of the tent.

Levi stepped back, a flush of embarrassment warming his cheeks. The woman had definitely heard him, so she wasn't hard of hearing. She simply wasn't interested in selling to him. Glancing around, he suddenly realized that many of the towns-folk in the area were steering clear of him. As they walked past, they curved their path so they left several feet of space between themselves and the boy.

The hat may have slightly concealed his face, but the people of Ainsworth weren't dull. They knew who he was, and if they placed their trust in the article Glenn showed him, they thought the Oakley family was to blame for every killing since Caroline.

Levi pulled the hat lower on his face and clutched the strap on the rucksack tighter. He didn't need someone to tell him outright. He knew he wasn't welcome there.

Keeping his head down, the boy quickly crossed to the other end of the market and headed toward the jail. He held his breath the entire walk, waiting for someone to stop him and tell him off. Or worse, for someone to take another swing at him. But no one approached as he walked to the other side of town. It wasn't until he turned down a side street that the boy finally released his breath and allowed himself to slow his pace.

While the market was bustling and full of shops, the roads on this side of town were mostly barren. The only structure around was a tall, wooden platform with a large beam rising from the center. Another plank extended outward from the top with a piece of rope hanging from the end of it. The rope was tied into a noose. Levi quickly focused back on the dirt beneath his feet, a shiver tracing down his spine.

At last, the boy came to a stop in front of the jailhouse. The building was one of the oldest in town, composed of weathered brick and a flat, angled roof. Two square windows framed either side of the wooden door, their views obscured by midnight blue curtains. If Levi craned his head, he could just make out the other side of the building that jutted out a bit further than the rest. A small, square hole near the top of the wall was covered with large metal bars running vertical to the building.

Ainsworth was a small town and didn't need too many cells. Levi was pretty sure they only had two or three at the most. The only time Levi had ever heard of someone being sent there for an extended period of time was after a man tried to rob a store and ended up shooting the owner when he tried to stop him. The sheriff kept him in the cell long enough to put him on trial, but he was eventually hung. Ma deemed Austin too young to see it at the time, but Pa took Levi to watch. The sight of the man's feet kicking and struggling before finally falling limp played in his mind every time he walked past the jailhouse and gallows.

The boy shook his head, forcing his mind off the memory, and creaked open the door to the jail.

Levi found himself in a small room, about the size of his home's kitchen. There was a woman seated at a table a few feet from the door, scribbling on a piece of paper. She glanced up when he entered and removed her glasses. Her brown hair was tied back tightly in a bun, but a few strands had fallen out and were tucked behind her ears. She seemed to be around Pa's age.

"Can I help you?" she asked.

Levi straightened up and made an expression he hoped appeared stern. "I'm here to see Sheriff Williams."

"He's quite busy," the woman replied, her eyes running over the boy. "Is there something you need?"

"Just tell him Levi Oakley is here to see him."

The woman hesitated, but eventually stood and left through the door on the other side of the room. Levi rocked back on his heels, cracking his knuckles and taking a few deep breaths in an attempt to quiet his nerves.

A few seconds later, the door swung open to reveal the sheriff. As soon as he recognized Levi, his expression darkened. "Why aren't you home?" he asked sharply.

"I'm sorry to disturb you," Levi quickly replied. "I just had a few questions I was hopin' you could answer for me." Williams gave him a look. The boy didn't want to reveal his leverage so early, but he realized the man might not talk to him any other way. "I also have… somethin' to tell you. About what happened to Jed?"

The man's eyes brightened and the corner of his mouth twitched. He ushered the boy inside. "I see. Come in."

As Levi stepped inside, he blinked in the sudden darkness. There were no lanterns and only a single window at the end of the hall cast light into the space. The shadow of the sheriff in front of him stretched along the floor, obscuring the scratched and marred planks of wood beneath their feet. They passed a few doors and finally stopped in front of a room on their left. A plaque nailed to the door read "Sheriff Paul Williams."

Based on the man's reputation for organization, Levi was expecting to find the office perfectly neat and tidy. But today, papers were haphazardly piled across the man's desk. A waste-basket in the corner was overflowing with rotten apple cores and dirty napkins. Now that Levi had started to notice, he also saw the hollowness of the man's cheeks and the redness rimming his eyes. The boy made all these observations silently as he crossed the room. While the sheriff moved to sit in the chair behind his desk, Levi remained standing.

Williams released a breath. "So," he asked once he was settled. "What do you have to tell me?"

Levi cleared his throat. Nervousness threatened to tremble his words, but he forced them steady. "I was actually hopin' you could answer my questions first. Then, I'll tell you what I know."

The sheriff narrowed his eyes, drumming his fingers on the desk. His gaze remained locked with Levi's. As the seconds dragged on, the boy became uneasy and itched to look away. But he felt like doing so would make him lose some sort of challenge. And he would never figure out what the sheriff knew.

"I'll allow it," Williams said finally and Levi hoped his exhale of relief was audible only to him.

"Thank you, sir." The boy swallowed past the dryness in his throat and asked, "Have you found anythin'? In the investigation, I mean."

It might've been Levi's imagination, but it seemed like the bags under the sheriff's eyes grew a shade darker. "We've had a few men walking through the town each night. Haven't reported anything of note – except, of course, those poor dead animals. Did you see that in the paper?" The man inspected Levi's expression as he nodded. He continued, "I put a group together to search the area. There was nothing out of the ordinary, at least that we could find."

"Did you find any animal tracks?"

Williams raised an eyebrow. "Not bear tracks, if that's what you're implying."

Levi tried to keep his expression stable, his heart sinking further. "So, my brother and I are still your only suspects."

"I'm afraid you are," the sheriff replied stiffly. Something about the way he said it told Levi he wasn't all that apologetic about the matter. Levi pursed his lips tightly, wishing he could tell the man what he really thought about the investigation's efforts – or lack thereof.

But Williams appeared oblivious to the boy's distress, for he sat back in his chair and folded his hands casually in front of him. "Anything else?"

"Well…" Levi trailed off, unsure of where to begin for his next point. "My brother and I were also wonderin' about what you and Pa were talkin' about when you were in the other room." The sheriff frowned and Levi quickly added, "We weren't eavesdroppin', promise. But… Pa mentioned our mother's name. Eloise. And we can't figure out why."

"Your mother's passing is not my business to discuss."

"But I think it's somehow related to what happened to Jed," Levi blurted. When the man across from him was silent, he rambled on, "Pa said somethin' strange – like, it's happenin' again. And he mentioned Ma's name. So, they have to be related. Or at least, he thinks they are. And… not to overstep, sir, but it sounded like Pa thought you knew what he was talkin' about. So, do you?"

The sheriff was silent for a moment. His gaze ran over Levi's face as if he was trying to decipher a puzzle. Again, Levi felt like he was being challenged. This time, though, he sat forward and met the man's questioning look with one of adamancy. The corner of William's eye twitched, but Levi refused to break the awkward quiet.

At last, the sheriff sniffed and gave the boy a smirk. "I suppose you're old enough to know. What I say next, you did not hear from me. Understand?"

Levi's breath caught in his chest. Whatever Williams had challenged him to, Levi had won. "Yessir."

The sheriff nodded, dropping his voice to a murmur. "Your father started acting… odd following the night your mother died. Not like a grieving widower would. He obsessed over the incident, telling everyone who would listen that he had seen a man in the woods that killed Eloise. We conducted a full search of your property and the surrounding woods, but nothing was found that would lead us to believe a person committed the crime.

"A few weeks later, your father assaulted a man in the town square. He claimed it was the man who killed your mother. I asked around and several stories corroborated the man to be working in the market at the time Eloise passed. Your father was arrested and I made him swear to never speak of the man again. Especially to you and your brother. We hoped he would set his delusions aside, focus on moving on and raising you boys properly.

"I told your father if I heard either of you discussing the man or asking strange questions about your mother's death, your farm would be taken over by the jurisdiction of the town." Levi's mouth dropped open, realizing what he had just done. "Don't worry," the sheriff assured him and the boy was surprised to see a hint of kindness enter his expression. "I don't plan on delivering on that promise, at least not at the moment. Things have gotten… more complicated with Jed's death. I'm not surprised this incident has brought these obsessions of your father back to life. When I was at your house last Friday, all I did was remind him of his promise to me. And what would happen if he didn't follow my orders. As long as he remains compliant, you have nothing to worry about."

Levi blinked, mind spinning with new information. "If you

don't think a man killed my mother, sir," he asked slowly, "then…
what do you think killed her?"

For the first time, Levi saw a crack in the man's stoic face. "I
didn't see her myself after it happened," he said softly. "And like
I said, it's not my place to speak on your mother's passing. But I
can tell you it was ruled an accident."

An accident. The sheriff didn't believe she had been murdered
– but he also never saw the body. He hadn't seen how much blood
coated her front, how pale her cheeks were in comparison. And
even though they never found any evidence of a murderer for
Eloise, they never found evidence for the recent killings, either.
That made another similarity between the events. But was a lack
of evidence between two incidents enough to prove that they
were connected?

It was only when Levi recognized the tense silence did he
realize Williams was waiting for a response. "Thank you, sir," he
responded curtly. "I won't speak a word of this to anyone."

The sheriff continued studying him. "Now," he said, and his
change of tone brought Levi's focus back to the present. "I feel as if
I've been more than fair answering your questions. Do you agree?"

Levi nodded. He had almost forgotten his promise. "Yessir."

"I'm glad we're on the same page. So, what did you come to
tell me?"

The boy took a moment to bide his time, weighing his words.
He wanted to tell the truth, but not in a way the man could use
against him. Even though Williams had shown some kindness
toward him, Levi still didn't fully trust him. "The other night, I
saw someone standin' outside the farm, facin' my window. They
were standin' real still, like I ain't never seen someone do before."

The sheriff pulled a pencil and empty sheet of paper from his
desk drawer. "Who was it?"

"I – uh, dunno."

"How tall were they?"

"I guess, maybe between five and six feet?"

"Hair color?"

"It was too dark to see."

"Age?"

"… I couldn't tell."

The pencil paused halfway across the page. "You just saw… someone."

"Yes, but…" How could he explain the sense of unease? The feeling that the person, whoever it was, was staring right at him? "I know it sounds like nothin'," Levi said hurriedly. "But for some reason I just feel like it's somehow related to my Pa and Eloise. The person was standin' strangely one minute and the next – they were gone."

Something flashed across the sheriff's face, too quick for Levi to catch. Williams sat forward, saying, "Don't worry, son. I believe you. Did this person… do anything?"

"No. He was just standin' there, then I looked away for a second and he disappeared."

"Is this the first time you've seen someone disappear? Or change in front of your eyes?"

Levi made a face. "Well, yeah. I ain't never seen anythin' like it."

"What about your brother? Has he ever mentioned seeing people you couldn't see?"

"No, he's never–" Levi froze. He stepped back, eyeing the man. "My family," he said slowly, "is *not* crazy."

Williams stood, holding up a hand. His expression remained perfectly apathetic. "I'm just trying to get all the facts here."

"You're tryin' to get me to admit that my brother and I are

seein' people that aren't there," Levi spat, his heart pounding in his ears. "Or that we killed Jed and all those animals. But I won't, because we didn't do any of those things." The boy gave the man one more withering look before turning toward the door. He had just pulled it open when–

"Jed wasn't just killed, Levi."

Levi stopped, his hand gripping the doorknob. He slowly looked back. "What?"

The man's eyes were dark. The pencil clutched in his hand seemed seconds away from snapping. "Jed wasn't just dead when we found him," he said. "There were deep cuts on his chest, down to the bone. Those horses you read about in the paper had them, too. They were all disemboweled."

Levi's blood ran cold. "I'm… sorry to hear that, sir."

"If I find a single ounce of proof that you or your family were involved in this, I swear I will make you rue the day you were born." Williams softened his face. "That is, unless you turn yourself in now. I might be able to waive some laws, forgo some procedures – and you might not be sent to the gallows. But only if you tell me exactly what happened the night that Lawson boy died."

The pair remained frozen for a long moment. Levi's fury boiled just below the surface, but he knew snapping back would only damage his case further. Instead, he bit his tongue and took a deep breath. "My brother and I had nothin' to do with it, sheriff," he answered coldly, "so we don't got nothin' to worry about. And we certainly ain't got nothin' to confess."

Williams crossed his arms over his chest. The muscles in his jaw tightened. "I'll be seeing you around, Levi."

Levi couldn't get out of the jailhouse fast enough. Once he made it to the end of the hallway, he burst in the room with the secretary, gave her a curt nod, and strode outside. After the cramped, dingy prison, he felt a surge of relief as fresh air filled his lungs. He trusted his feet to walk him back home without the help of his conscious mind. His thoughts were a blur, dissecting every word the sheriff said.

He knew for certain now – they were after Levi's family. It wasn't just a rumor anymore. Williams was actively searching for evidence that would incriminate them. And Levi might've accidentally given him something he could use against them by mentioning the mysterious figure in his backyard. But if he did, why didn't the sheriff just arrest him right there?

It still must not have been enough, Levi realized. Williams might have his own suspicions, but it still wasn't enough to throw him and his family in a cell.

A man. There was a man there the night Ma died. Or at least, that's what Pa thought he saw. Could it be the same person that Levi saw standing outside his window? But Ma died years ago, and he saw the figure just a few nights ago. The person would have to be older now, much older. And then there was the fact that the sheriff never found any evidence of a murder at the scene of Ma's death. But they never found any evidence for the animal's deaths, or Jed's.

At least he knew one thing for certain, now: why Pa was arrested. It wasn't some random person Pa attacked. The person looked similar to whoever Pa saw near the woods. That was probably why he wanted his sons to keep away from the treeline, too. Who knew what could be lurking in the trees that the sheriff and the rest of the town had overlooked?

And what the sheriff said about Jed and the horses, how they were *disemboweled*… whoever committed these crimes didn't have an ounce of humanity in them. They were striking out randomly and savagely, without hesitation.

I'm not gonna wait for the sheriff to figure all this out, Levi decided as he crested the hill and approached the farm. He was going with Austin to the forest tonight with the sole purpose of searching for the figure, or any sign that someone was living in the woods. A part of him hoped they found nothing aside from wild animals among the trees. But his curiosity longed to get a better look at the figure that was stalking Ainsworth for who knew how long.

At least then he would know for sure if he really had been dreaming that night.

Levi knew that Austin would have an irritating amount of questions when he returned to the farm and the boy didn't disappoint. Over the course of several hours, he pestered his older brother with inquiries of what happened, if something was wrong, and if he found out anything. Levi evaded his interrogations, assuring his younger brother he would explain after supper.

Even with his morning spent in the market and the sheriff's office, there were still a few hours left in the day for work. Austin had finished reinforcing the fence when Levi arrived back and together they worked on the remainder of the chores. Due to Levi's time spent in the market, things went slower than usual and the two ended up skipping over self-defense lessons and their free time to ensure everything was taken care of. Just as the sun began to set, Levi went to the chicken coop for the last task of the day. As he cleaned and gathered the day's supply of eggs, he subconsciously glanced over his shoulder every few seconds. Though the shadowy figure was nowhere in sight, as night approached, the boy felt his anxiousness growing. He picked up his pace and made sure to lock the coop tight and wave Austin inside before night had fully fallen.

While Levi cooked supper for the evening, Austin sat at the table and pretended to read a book. Every few seconds, he would steal a look at his older brother. Levi ignored him, focusing his attention on the meal. His brother's probing expression was quite clear, but Levi had to wait for the right moment. He wasn't about to start talking and have their father interrupt them as they made a plan to explore the outskirts of the treeline. Austin would have to be patient.

When the meal was ready a few minutes later, Levi made three plates and set them all at the kitchen table. Austin scarfed his down without hesitation and proceeded to shoot daggers with his eyes as his older brother slowly cleared his portion. Once Levi sat back in his chair, the two brothers turned to look at their father's heaping plate.

They sat there in silence for one long minute.

Then, Levi sighed. "Austin."

Austin's head swiveled to look at him. He knew what that tone of voice meant: *it's time.* "Yeah?"

"Bring Pa's supper up to him. Knock on the door and if he don't answer, leave it outside. Don't forget utensils."

Austin nodded enthusiastically and scurried around the table to grab the plate, fork, and knife. While he rushed up the stairs, Levi stood and lifted the oil lamp from the side table. He also grabbed his flannel jacket off the hook next to the door and pulled it on. As Austin came back down the stairs, he instantly smiled when he saw Levi with his jacket on. He tried to rush past him to grab his own, but Levi grabbed his arm to stop him. "Don't smile," he said sharply. "This ain't nothin' to laugh about."

Austin shrugged out of his grip, rolling his eyes. "I'm just happy we're finally doin' somethin' is all."

"Keep your voice down." Levi glanced toward the staircase. All seemed quiet, so he said, "When I talked to Williams today, I learned a few things. He told me that the day Ma was killed, Pa saw a man nearby. By the woods."

Austin's eyes widened. "A man? Did he give her the berries?"

"I don't think there ever were berries." Levi paused while he gathered his thoughts. "The sheriff never found any proof of a murder and Ma's death was ruled an accident. But we know Jed was killed – maybe by a bear, maybe somethin' else – but there wasn't any evidence found there, either. Which makes me think they're connected. If this is the same person that killed Jed, they've been doin' this a long time. Ma died nearly a decade ago and now they're killin' again, both times without leavin' a shred of evidence behind."

"So, what're we gonna do?"

"You and I are headed to the woods and we're gonna see what we can find. Maybe we'll find the man Pa thought he saw, or the figure outside the house." Levi's expression sombered. "We gotta figure out whether Pa can be trusted, whether he actually saw what he thought he saw. If there ain't nothin' there, we might have to start considerin' that Pa… might not be in the right state 'a mind."

"You really think Pa can't be trusted?"

Levi pursed his lips. "Williams told me somethin' else today. Pa was arrested because he attacked a man. He thought the man killed Ma, but he ended up bein' wrong, and they threw him in jail overnight." Levi saw his brother's expression and said, "I'm not sayin' for sure that Pa is wrong about all this. Maybe Pa and I are just seein' things. But if the person that killed Jed and maybe

Ma is still here, I think he's somewhere in those woods. And we need to find him before he hurts anyone else."

Levi stood and strode to the far wall, where his father's guns hung on the wall. Carefully, with both hands, he lifted a rifle off its hooks. He turned back toward his brother. "We're not doin' this just for fun, or to solve a mystery. We're doin' this to save our family."

Austin stared wide-eyed at the weapon, then looked to the staircase as if Pa could sense his precious firearm being touched without his permission. But the house remained silent. If their father was awake, he showed no sign of it.

The two brothers exchanged a glance and Levi nodded. Austin scampered to the opposite side of the room to pull on his coat and lace up his boots. All the while, Levi listened carefully for any sign of movement upstairs. By the time his brother was ready to leave, he was certain their father was asleep for the night.

Levi led the way, quietly opening the front door and stepping onto the porch. He dimmed his lantern as much as possible without snuffing it out completely and covered the side of it that faced the house. The pair quickly strode up the side of the hill using the light of the moon to avoid tripping. They kept to the shadows, lest Pa decided to look out the window at the wrong moment. Levi knew the path well, the way being burned into his mind ever since Caroline was taken. Once they were out of the shadow of the barn and into the open moonlight, they sped up to a light jog until they reached the crest of the hill.

Only when they were completely out of sight of the house did Levi turn up the brightness of the lamp and crouch down to start examining the ground. At first glance, there didn't seem to be anything out of the ordinary.

"The marks are still here from Caroline," Levi muttered. "A bit more faded now."

"Should we follow them?"

Without replying, Levi began walking slowly in the direction the tracks were facing. After a few steps, he stopped and pointed down. "Look. That one's fresh."

Austin squinted at it. "That don't look like a bear print, though."

"You're right." Levi crouched down, running his hand along the indentation in the mud. "It ain't as deep, and smaller. Looks more like a fox, or a small dog."

"They're both headed to the forest."

The two tracks branched off in slightly different directions, but it was clear they had the same destination. Levi thought for a moment and turned to the left. "Let's follow the fresher tracks. We'll have a better chance at seein' somethin'."

"But we ain't lookin' for a dog, we're lookin' for a person."

"I don't see no human tracks right now, so we might as well follow the ones we've got in front of us."

When Austin couldn't come up with a rebuttal, the pair began walking toward the treeline. They kept their heads down, careful not to muddle any of the tracks with their steps.

"Wait a minute," Levi whispered suddenly. He spun around. "Where'd it go?"

Austin stepped forward, also staring at the ground. "The prints just stopped."

Backtracking, Levi again found the prints. And then – nothing. They didn't jump ahead or continue into the trees. They were still a few feet from the shrubbery. The older brother crouched down, pressing his fingers into the soil ahead and behind the last visible print. "The ground feels the same," he said. "So if it made a print here it shoulda made it ahead, too."

"Did it jump into the woods?"

"Not from this far." Levi glanced around. "It's like it just vanished midstride."

The younger brother was forming a response when a scream rang out. Both boys shot to their feet and Levi raised the gun to eye-level toward the source of the sound. "It came from the woods," Austin whispered, his voice trembling. He picked up the oil lamp and held it out, but it didn't cast light further than a few feet ahead of them.

Another scream, closer this time. The voice sounded masculine, but slightly pitched. A chill radiated down Levi's spine and his heart pounded wildly in his chest. He squinted his eyes, but much as he tried, he couldn't make any sense of the shadows among the trees. The gun trembled in his hands and he gripped it tighter to steady it. He wasn't dreaming this time. Whatever was making that noise was real.

Austin turned to Levi with wide eyes. "Whaddya think–"

"*Help!*" The boys instantly stepped back and Levi flipped the safety off of the gun, training it on the trees. The voice sounded like it was no more than a few yards in front of them, but even as the boy blinked and squinted his eyes, he found only darkness between the leaves. Levi wracked his brain, the sound being familiar in some way, he just couldn't–

"*Please, help me!*" It seemed like the voice was coming from all directions, pressing in on them and filling their minds. Levi's legs were weak beneath him and he had to force himself to hold his ground.

"What do we do?" Austin gasped, taking a step toward the trees.

"Don't move," snapped Levi. He kept the barrel of the gun trained ahead of them. "It could be a trap."

"But someone needs help!" Austin paused, squinting toward the forest. "It sounds – sounds like…"

"I'm beggin' you! It's me!"

Both boys froze as the realization hit. "It sounds like a kid," breathed Levi.

Suddenly, Levi felt a sharp pain at his ear. The force dragged him backward and he pulled the weapon to his chest to stop him from dropping it. Austin cried out and Levi saw him being pulled too, away from the forest and back in the direction of the house. Levi spun around and found himself in the grasp of a tall, broad figure. "Pa," he gasped, reaching for his ear with one hand and trying to rip away from the man's hold. "There's someone out there, we gotta–"

"There ain't no one out there," barked the man. He adjusted his grip to grab the boys' collars and continued striding forward. The pair scrambled to keep up as they clutched the man's hands.

"But you gotta have heard him," hissed Austin. "He was screamin' for his life! What if he's with the guy that killed Jed?"

Pa stopped and shoved both boys forward. They stumbled, but didn't fall. Their shoulders were heaving with frantic, terrified breaths.

The three of them stood there for a moment, staring at each other in the flickering light of the oil lamp.

Pa's gaze stopped on the weapon Levi was clutching. His eyes narrowed and he wordlessly held out his hands. There was a second of hesitation before the boy handed over the gun. Levi closed his eyes, knowing what was likely to follow.

The slap whipped across his cheek, its impact forcing him a step back. Levi raised his head to look at his father, ignoring his stinging face. Pa's jaw tightened as he slung the gun over his shoulder. He cleared his throat, spitting a glob of mucus into the dusty soil. "Listen to me very carefully," the man snarled. He had the boys' full attention now. "You did not *hear* anythin' in that forest. You did not *see* anythin' in that forest. If I see either of you goin' near that place ever again, I swear to Christ I will tie you down like hogs and beat you numb. Is that understood?"

"But Pa…" Austin trailed off when he saw his father glance at him, and he quickly added, "Yessir." A moment of silence passed without Levi's reply, and both man and boy turned to look at him. He stood stock still, staring at his father with a dark expression.

"Is what I said understood, boy?" muttered Pa.

Levi took a breath. He had been silent long enough. He needed to say something now, especially with what he knew. "Animals are gettin' killed," he said softly. "A boy was slaughtered and everyone thinks we're the ones that did it. They're huntin' us down, startin' brawls in the market…" The boy paused to gather himself. "We can't let the sheriff stop us from keepin' our farm safe, not when whoever is doin' these killin's is still loose."

The boy winced in anticipation, waiting for another flourish of pain. But instead, his father just looked at him.

"Son," Pa whispered, his face taut with emotion. Although his expression didn't change, Levi saw his eyes flicker. He saw anger, pity… and something that looked like grief. It was possible he understood that Levi had acquired new information, but if he did, he didn't act on it. Then, his face crumbled back into the sharp, expressionless face Levi had seen for most of his life. "Is what I said understood?" the man asked.

Whatever moment the older brother had witnessed was gone. The boy straightened his back, steeled his shoulders. He, too, put on his own emotionless mask and stared blankly at his father. "Yessir."

Pa gave the boys one last, long look before walking back toward the house. Although Austin's eyes lingered on his brother's face, he quickly followed behind their father. But Levi hesitated.

He turned to stare back into the forest, analyzing each rustling leaf and fleeting shadow. Whatever had just been screaming for help was silent now. There was no mistaking that for a dream – there was definitely someone out there. And the way Pa reacted when he saw them… it was like he was expecting something to happen when they got near the woods.

There was so much that still didn't make sense. Caroline's murder couldn't have been done by a human, no one was strong enough to tear down the fence like that. And the tracks in the field were certainly an animal's, not a human's. So either there was a murderer and a rogue animal running loose in Ainsworth…

Or they were somehow the same.

"Levi!" The boy turned to see his younger brother gesturing for him to hurry. "C'mon, before Pa gets mad again."

Levi nodded once and started walking back toward the house. He felt like he had more information, but was no closer to answers. Was there possibly someone dead in the forest, now? Should he report it to Williams?

No, he decided. If there was someone dead out there, the last thing he needed was to lead Williams to the body. That would be more than enough evidence for their arrest. He wasn't relying on the sheriff or Ainsworth any longer. Williams might be able to stop Pa from figuring out what was really going on, but he had no power over Levi and Austin.

Chapter Eight

L EVI SPENT THE night staring at his ceiling, carefully thinking over each piece of information he had acquired. It was clear now: even though Pa might be right about a human being involved with this, Levi was now almost certain the thing they were looking for wasn't entirely human. Or at least, a kind of human they were familiar with. That's why they had so much trouble determining exactly what they were looking for.

Levi also kept recalling the fact that Pa had been there the night before. He had heard what Austin and Levi heard in the woods – and it still wasn't enough to make him act. Even when the evidence stared him in the face, Williams' threat was enough to keep him from doing something about it. That meant the scheming was up to Levi.

He had some money from his sales in the market earlier that week, but if he was to get enough for a weapon, he would need to sell out of all his stock on Monday and keep at least half the profits for himself. He'd need to come up with a plausible reason for the lack of cash in case his father asked, but it was a risk he would have to take. He'd also have to hope that the gunsmith in town was willing to sell to Levi at all. After what he experienced in the market, he wasn't sure anyone in Ainsworth was on his family's side. But he'd have to try.

Next, he needed to determine exactly what he was up against. If he could assume that all the attacks in town were committed by the same killer, whatever it was had killed a cow, a dog, several horses, and a person (or possibly two, if Ma was included). If that figure Levi had seen outside the coop a few days back wasn't a dream, then whatever it was could look like a person and apparently sound like one, too. Maybe something that was part animal, part human? More human than animal, though – it was able to speak with such clarity. He didn't know exactly what to keep an eye out for, anything or anyone was potentially a threat.

Finally, he needed a way to prove to the town that he and his brother weren't behind all this. He wasn't sure how much longer Williams would stand down, but if it was being written about in the paper, word was going to travel fast. Even if Levi said he killed it, he would need proof for them to believe him.

To complete the first step of his plan, he had to wait much longer than he would've preferred. If today was Saturday, that meant he had to wait a full two days before he could get any more money for the weapon on Monday. Until then, he needed to lull his father into a false sense of security that he was content staying on the farm. When the time was right and Pa wasn't watching, he would make his move. For a moment, he considered stealing the money from his father in order to purchase the gun faster. He could probably afford one now if he used all of the money they made at the market on Monday and Wednesday, but he had his own reservations about stealing, even in a high-stakes situation such as this one.

The next day, the boys started their routine per usual. At least, they tried. Austin dropped and shattered a plate during breakfast. When Levi went to open the gate and let the herd loose, they flooded out and nearly trampled him. He watched them dart around the field, desperate for the open air. It seemed like everything on the farm coursed with energy, ready to snap at a moment's notice.

For several hours, the brothers exchanged as few words as possible with each other. They took care of the animals, churned butter, and tidied the interior of the house. All the while, the shadow of their father loomed in the top-most window of the house, watching like a hawk.

There was no sign of the creature, human or animal. Whenever Levi had a spare minute or was catching his breath, he glanced toward the woods, almost willing something to appear. But nothing ever did. Whoever they had heard that night didn't return. Or if it did, it never showed its face when Levi was staring between the tree trunks.

Sometime throughout the day, the boy felt a sharp pain start in his temple. He was unsure whether it was caused by either the glaring sun or the looming sense of dread, but neither of them he was able to remedy anytime soon. It slowly crescendoed with each passing minute, beginning as a minor annoyance and increasing to a stabbing on the right side of his head.

As Levi was gathering water for dinner, a shadow darted overhead. He looked up to find a large, dark bird gliding over the farm. He followed its path with his eyes and saw it was moving toward the forest. And it wasn't the only one. There were at least five of them flying over something in the middle of the woods. Levi watched as the bird flew into the group and began circling the same location. He squinted at it before lifting the bucket of water and taking it inside. Birds that size weren't an uncommon occurrence around the woods, but something about seeing that many together set his teeth on edge.

As Levi made supper, he couldn't quell the feeling that the walls were closing in on him. His heart thumped in his chest like he was sprinting. His headache was splitting and any bright light made him wince in pain. When his brother entered the room, he jumped and nearly cut himself while chopping potatoes. Austin gave him a look, but said nothing.

After he and Austin ate, Levi shut his eyes and massaged the sides of his head. If he was going to survive the next few days, he needed to pull himself together. He had a plan, he just needed to be patient before he could act.

And pray that no one else was killed in the meantime.

"What's wrong?"

Levi blearily looked at his brother across the table.

"Nothin'. My head just hurts."

"Alright," Austin replied, then went back to staring at his plate.

"Actually," Levi said as the idea struck him. "Could you take a plate of grub up to Pa? I'm gonna take a walk and clear my head."

Austin glanced toward the orange glow coming from the kitchen window. "The sun is setting. Pa don't want us out when it's dark."

Levi stood. "I know, I'll be back before it's dark."

His little brother didn't seem fully convinced, but at that point, Levi didn't care. He just needed to get out of the house.

As Levi stepped outside, the sunset lit farm was still and quiet. He breathed deeply, letting his shoulders drop and releasing some of the tension they'd been holding the past few days. This was just what he needed, a few minutes to himself.

He stepped onto the dirt, headed toward the open field. He passed the chicken coop, the barn within which he heard the sounds of the rustling herd, and arrived at the edge of the fence. Although Levi hadn't exactly known where he was going when he first decided to go for a walk, now it seemed so obvious what he needed at that moment.

Instead of heading straight over the hill and to the forest, he continued around the outskirts of the fence until he was walking parallel to the darkening trees. The sun was lowering to his left, burning the sky in bright hues of red and orange. As he grew closer, he saw a rounded stone jutting out from the dull green grass and dusty ground.

Levi stopped a few feet from the headstone. Even though he knew the inscription by heart, he read it again, drinking in each word like it held answers to the countless questions suffocating his mind.

ELOISE OAKLEY

WIFE OF CLINT OAKELY

BORN MAY 17, 1843

DIED APRIL 19, 1871

The headstone was almost a decade old, but it was still in excellent condition. There was hardly a speck of dirt on it and the grass around the grave was kept well trimmed and taken care of, courtesy of Pa. It was like he was making up for the lost time with his wife while she was living by tending to every detail of her resting place.

The boy shifted his weight, crossing his arms in front of him. When he was little, he used to talk to his mother's grave: tell her how his day was, if Austin was irritating him, when he got a good grade on an exam. He hadn't done it in years, but for some reason, he felt the words desperately asking to be spoken aloud.

"Hey, Ma," he said quietly. "I'm sure you've been seein' all the… stuff goin' on down here."

Levi waited as if his mother would reply. But the only answer he received was in the rustling of weeds and faint bird calls. The boy swallowed and began again.

"I'm tryin' to do my best. There's somethin' goin' on and I just feel like I'm not doin' enough about it, or I'm not goin' about it the right way. I'm missin' somethin'. And… I think it has somethin' to do with you."

Levi shut his eyes for a moment, forcing his voice to stay even. "I wish I was there that day. Not just to see you, but to see what happened with my own eyes. Pa has his reasons for hidin' the truth from us, even if I don't fully understand it. But with him not bein' honest, I'm not sure who we can trust."

The tip of the sun dipped below the horizon. While the sky still held hints of pinks and oranges, dark blue was beginning to seep through. His time was running short.

"I'm not sure what it's like up there," Levi whispered, lifting his gaze to the watercolor sky, "but if you're able to send us some help – or give us a sign – I'd really appreciate it."

A gust of wind blew through the clearing, pressing down the strands of grass. It seemed to kiss his cheek as it went by.

Levi smiled. "Thanks, Ma," he whispered. The boy dipped his hat, then turned back toward home.

As Levi approached the house, he immediately noticed something was off. Frenzied shadows moved behind the windows, dashing from one side of the kitchen to the other. He picked up the pace, suddenly becoming aware of how much the sky had changed in the last few minutes. The sun was completely set now and hazy shadows were blanketing the land.

When he was a few feet away from the door, it swung open, revealing a figure standing in the doorway. Levi skid to a halt. "Glenn?" he asked. "What're you doin' here?'

Glenn's face was pale, his eyes wide and frantic. His shoulders were heaving with exertion, but he was able to pant, "I – came to warn you. Someone died this morning. Mrs. Franklin. Sheriff found her body close to dawn."

Levi's stomach dropped. "Why didn't you tell me sooner?"

"I woulda," Glenn replied breathily, "but my Pa wouldn't let me outta the house once he heard the news. He don't think the town is safe no more. I'm supposed to be tendin' to the flock, but I ran off the farm as soon as he wasn't lookin'."

Levi took a breath, forcing a stoic expression on his face. "I... I'll have the gun by Monday night. We can find this thing next week and–"

"You don't understand." Glenn straightened and stepped closer to Levi. The terrified glint in his eyes made Levi's words die on his lips. "My Pa also said he overheard people talkin' when he went into town this mornin'. Some boys are comin' for you. Tonight."

"What, they want another fight or somethin'?"

The boy shook his head. "Not a fight. I heard them gatherin' alcohol, matches – and guns."

Levi's blood ran cold. "And they're comin' for us?"

Glenn nodded shakily. "Jesse and Cole convinced half the school you're a murderer, Levi. And not just that, but they've come up with all sorts of stories about you and your family. That your dad is a psycho, that he killed your Ma–"

"What?" Levi's fists clenched at his sides, his voice tightening. "There's no way any of them believe that... do they?"

"Some of them just go along with it so they're not the next

target. But I think a lot of them do at this point. And us not bein' in school, you have no way to defend yourself. Or prove to others that you weren't there for Jed's killin' or any of the others. Anythin' bad goin' on in town they're blamin' on you. And people are gettin' fed up."

Levi closed his eyes, forcing his lungs to take full, deep breaths. But his mind wouldn't work, couldn't think. It kept playing back the same five words in his mind: *They're comin' for you. Tonight.* "Have you told Austin and my Pa yet?"

"I told Aus, I didn't see your Pa. I told your brother to find him."

Just then, Austin's small frame appeared in the doorway behind Glenn.

"Levi!" called Austin, his voice shrill with emotion. "Pa's gone!"

Levi stared at him. "Waddya mean, gone?"

"He's not anywhere on the farm. I checked the house, the barn, the shed – I even knocked on his study. And his huntin' rifle ain't on the wall."

Levi's eyes went wide. "He musta heard about the killin' this mornin', too," he realized. "He took the gun and went to hunt down whatever is causin' all this."

"Where do you think he went?" asked Glenn.

Levi glanced at the tips of the trees looming over the far hill. "I have an idea."

Austin followed his gaze toward the woods. "You really think he went in there?"

"He seemed to have a better idea of what was causin' all this than anyone else. And he knew it had somethin' to do with the forest. Williams held him back from doin' anythin' for a long time, but the threat of the boys comin' for us must've finally been enough for him to take action."

"Why is Williams' holdin' him back?" Glenn said.

Levi opened his mouth but hesitated, realizing just how much he had yet to tell his friend. "It's a long story, I'll catch you up later. For now, we've got work to do." He shoved past his brother and strode to the far wall. Just as Austin had said, the hooks that usually held their father's hunting rifle were empty. However, a smaller rifle that he normally let Austin and Levi practice with was still there, in addition to two Remington revolvers. Levi pulled one of them off the wall and checked if it was loaded.

"What work?" Austin asked, staring over Levi's shoulder. "Wait, you're takin' Pa's guns? He's gonna kill you."

"We need protection," Levi responded evenly. "Pa would understand if he was here." He cocked the rifle and heard the bullet slide into place. "Glenn, take a Remington and keep lookout by the front door. I gotta put a few things together before we go."

Glenn nodded, grabbing the weapon and moving to stand on the front steps. Once the door closed behind him, Levi pulled his rucksack off the kitchen table and started shoving things inside. Some food, his knife, a jacket, anything that might even have a small chance of coming in useful in the woods. All the while, his brother followed him like a shadow.

"What're we gonna do?"

"We're gonna look for Pa and the thing that's causin' these killin's and hope we find Pa first."

"You think we're lookin' for a person or an animal?"

"I'm not sure. We saw tracks by the forest but heard a person screamin', so I'm thinkin' this is somethin' neither of us have seen before."

"You think Pa knows what he's lookin' for?"

"I dunno, probab…" Levi trailed off, pausing with a compass

clutched in one hand. His father might not know exactly what was out there, but he definitely knew more about it than anyone else in Ainsworth. And since he wasn't in the house, they might have a chance of finding out just what their father was hiding. "If he does," the boy said slowly, "he might have somethin' about it in his study."

Austin's eyes widened when he realized his brother's idea and both boys slowly turned toward the staircase. Levi closed the rucksack and stepped up the stairs, Austin following close behind. The house was eerily quiet. Not a single lantern was lit and the walls were drenched in shadow. When Levi put his hand on the doorknob that led to his father's study, he couldn't help but hesitate. Even though he knew Pa wasn't in the house, it still felt wrong to intrude on his space. In the end, however, it was easier asking forgiveness than permission, even from a father that might've lost his mind. Levi took a breath, pushed aside his unease, and opened the door. As the pair stepped inside, their eyes went wide.

"My God," breathed Austin.

The room was covered in papers. Some contained drawings, others scrawled writing. They were tacked, nailed, even glued to the walls. Levi spun around, seeing the article that Glenn had given him about the horses was among the fray. There were books about fighting techniques and the quickest way to disarm an adversary. Other pages were covered in manic scribbles that the boy couldn't make out.

Something caught Levi's eye and he pointed across the room. "There! The missin' article from the library."

Plucking it off the wall, Austin skimmed over it. "He must've had it this whole time," he muttered. "Don't say anythin' about a man, though, or about the forest. Just says she died under mysterious circumstances." He paused and added, "It don't even say anythin' about her gettin' poisoned."

Levi pursed his lips, gritted his teeth. So his father really had been lying to them all these years, since the very first day Ma passed. His roaming eyes stopped on one particular drawing pinned to a wall. He quickly strode to it and tore it off. Holding it up to his face, his heart dropped as he realized what he was looking at. It was a hand-drawn sketch of a person standing next to the chicken coop. The angle was different from when Levi had witnessed it, but he recognized it right away. It was the same figure Levi had seen that night from his bedroom window. When the boy looked closer, he saw his father had been able to catch some details of the figure that he hadn't. The strange shape around the person's hips wasn't a skirt, but a collection of round patches of fur – pelts. And the figure's face was also more distinct in the drawing, more recognizable. It was–

"Jed." Levi turned the paper over to show Austin. "The figure I saw that night was Jed. Or at least, Pa seems to think it was."

Austin's eyes flicked from the drawing to his brother. "But Jed's dead."

"I know."

His younger brother had lost some color in his face. "You think it was a ghost?"

"No." Levi turned the paper back over and stared into the face of his dead classmate. "Jed's gone. It coulda been any number of kids. All this confirms is that Pa really was losin' his mind." He glanced around the room, taking in the maddening scribbles and sketches. "I'm not sure we can trust any of this as fact."

Austin stared at Levi with wide eyes. "But if you saw him too, don't that make you crazy?"

"I saw a person outside my window. I sure as hell didn't see a dead person." Levi noticed his brother's expression and rolled his eyes. "C'mon, I haven't lost my mind. I told you I saw a person. I didn't see Jed. Whatever Pa saw is his own business."

Austin nodded but didn't look entirely convinced. "What if Amos was wrong?" he asked. "What if Jed somehow survived?"

"You saw the way Amos was actin' at school. I don't think he woulda mistaken him for dead if he was alive." Levi crumpled the paper in his hand. "All of this is useless. Pa's mind was gone, we're no closer to solvin' any of this."

Austin was quiet. Then, he whispered, "What's that on his desk?"

Levi turned toward where his brother was pointing. Pa's writing desk was covered in papers like the rest of the space, but a small, brown, book spine peaked out between a few sheets. The older brother strode over, shoved the haphazard pages aside and picked up the journal. He quickly leafed through it, skimming as he went.

"He used it to keep records for the farm," he explained. "Crop rotations, weather…" He paused and flipped back a few pages. "Wait a minute…"

Austin stepped closer to look over his shoulder. "What is it?"

"He wrote somethin' in the corner," Levi muttered. "I think it says *change*." He turned to the next page, and there it was again, this time in between entries describing the weather. *Change.* But there were other words written there, too. *Eloise* and *It's watching me.* The boy ran his thumb over an indentation in the paper, and when he flipped it over, he breathed, "Christ Almighty."

The page was covered in writing. Words were layered over each other, pressing into the page and smearing the graphite. Certain phrases were written over and over again, overlapping and making permanent indents into the paper. Levi searched for whatever coherent words he could find among the chaos.

ELOisE my LoVE ELoisE
I have changes ChANGe It kills KiLL it
have to kill it I must kill it
It's watching me The woods
her Don'T BELievE me
BlooOD
iT Lives iN The woods
It's coming for me It's comii
FoR us It knows They're watching me
iT Lives iN The woods
They cAn't StOP Me
iT Lives iN The woods
It KNoWS whERe WE liVe
HELp Me
God I have to stop it.
IT's NotSAf

Levi's hands shook as he turned the book to show his brother. "The entry is dated for today," he said softly.

Austin's eyes went wide, taking in the frantic scribbles. "What does he mean?" he whispered. *"It changes?"*

His older brother thought for a moment. "I've heard that phrase before." After a few seconds, he remembered. "Williams asked me somethin' similar when I was in his office. He asked me if I had seen people *change*." His eyes brightened, finally feeling like he was making some sense of all this. "That must be what Pa told him to make him think he was crazy. He must've thought the man that killed Ma *changed*."

Austin nodded slowly, trying his best to keep up. "Have you seen anyone change?"

"No. I don't even know what it means." The boy looked around the room. "He's been keepin' a record of everythin', from the day Ma passed."

Austin remained focused on the journal. "All this time," he murmured, "I thought he was just sleepin' the days away. But he was gatherin' information faster than we were."

"He did have a few years head start."

Austin pointed to a paper that had fallen to the floor. "There." He crouched down and picked it up. "It's a drawin' of different pelts," he described. "They're labeled: fox, rabbit, dog. There's a feather labeled bird."

"The drawin' of Jed had him wearin' pelts, too," Levi said. He felt like he could spend hours in the room, assembling the puzzle. The answers were in here, somewhere. But they didn't have hours to spare. Without another word, Levi hustled past Austin and pounded down the stairs.

"Wait!" he heard Austin call from behind him. "Where're you goin'?"

"I'm goin' after Pa." Once Levi made it to the kitchen, he pulled the bag off his shoulder and shoved a handful of ammo inside. He threw open the front door. "Any sign of them?" he asked Glenn.

The boy shook his head, still seated on the step. "Did you find anythin'?"

"I'll let Austin explain," Levi said before striding out into the field.

"Wait a minute," Glenn hissed, following closely behind. "Where're you goin'?"

"Into the woods. I'm findin' Pa. Stay here with Austin, guard the farm."

"No!" Austin pushed past Glenn and glared at Levi. "I'm not stayin' here."

"Yeah, you are."

"I'm comin' with you."

"No, you're not."

"It's my farm, too!"

"That's why you need to protect it."

"Then, you protect it!"

"Enough." Levi took off again, but–

"Levi!"

The older brother turned to look at his sibling. Austin had a tear tracing down his left cheek.

Levi's heart went out to him. The boy just found out he had been lied to by his father for years, there was a mysterious creature attacking the people and animals of Ainsworth, and his brother was about to go into the woods his father just ran into.

And he had no idea if either would return.

"Please, Aus," Levi said evenly. "I know this is hard. But I dunno what's goin' happen out there. I'm responsible for you and I can't let Pa down... or Ma."

Austin blinked. More tears fell. He angrily wiped them away before meeting his brother's eyes. "I already lost Ma. I can't l-lose both of you, too."

Levi felt his throat tighten, but he kept his expression neutral. He wanted to wrap his brother in his arms, tell him it was gonna be fine, that they could go home and forget the woods, go back to the way things used to be. But he knew that was impossible. He also knew if he took the time to comfort his brother the way he wanted to, he wouldn't have the strength to leave. Instead, he stepped up to Austin and put a hand on his shoulder. "Listen to me," he said. "If things don't… work out tonight, I need you to promise you'll take care of the farm. I *will* kill whatever is out there. But if it takes me down with it, someone needs to tend to our herd."

Austin shook his head, squeezing his eyes shut. "Don't say that. You're – you're comin' back. With Pa."

"I'll do everythin' I can." Levi grasped his brother's arm tighter. "But you have to promise me. If things go south."

Austin was silent as tears continued streaming down his cheeks. But when he looked up, his eyes were alight with purpose. "I p-promise."

Levi looked at him for a moment longer, then nodded. "I'll be seein' you, Aus," he whispered. Austin nodded, stepping away to wipe at his face again. Levi tipped his head to his friend. "Take care of my brother, Glenn."

The boy nodded. "I will. Be safe out there. And kill that son of a bitch."

A half smile, half grimace crept across Levi's face. "I'll do my best."

As Levi strode away from the house, he waited until he was over the hill and out of sight to wipe the moisture from his eyes. He was just as scared and unsure of himself as his brother was, but he couldn't let Austin see it. He needed his brother to believe there was some hope in all of this.

There was a waning moon that night and its glow cut through the darkness like a knife. The trees rose taller the closer Levi got, their points biting into the starry night sky. Right when Levi got to the edge of the bushes, he paused, listening for any sound or movement. The leaves rustled gently in the breeze. The cricket song that would usually lull him to sleep sounded like a warning, pleading with him to turn back.

He paused and looked back in the direction of the farm. This was it. The moment he was stepping out of the familiar and into the unknown. He didn't fully know what was out there. All he knew was whatever it was had already taken so much from him. He wouldn't – no, *couldn't* – let it take anyone else.

Levi took a shaky breath, steeling his shoulders.

Then, he moved into the forest.

Chapter Nine

D URING THE FIRST few minutes of walking, the trees were more spaced out than Levi expected. The moonlight streamed through the branches and lit the path in front of him as if guiding his way. A slight breeze rustled the leaves, but the sound was mostly concealed by the continuing cricket song. He strode confidently, keeping his priorities at the forefront of his mind. His steps were paced to his thoughts: *Find my father. Kill the creature. Find my father. Kill the creature.*

But as the minutes passed, the pale, natural light became obstructed by the canopy of leaves and branches overhead. It was difficult to navigate the forest without a lamp, and he tripped over several rocks and above-ground roots before finally pausing. He turned around, back toward the farm. He couldn't see home from where he was standing, but he thought he could just make out the line where the trees ended and the prairie began. However, if he was being honest, it could've just been his eyes playing tricks on him, transforming shadows into shapes that weren't actually there.

Levi raised his eyebrows, opening his eyes as wide as he could. They were adjusting to his surroundings, but not quickly enough.

While he waited, he undid the buckles on his bag and pulled out the compass. Home was east. But even with knowing the cardinal direction, he needed a more easily identifiable way of getting home if things went awry, something he could spot from a distance away if he was in a hurry or the compass broke. He thought for a moment, then clicked open his knife.

Levi turned around to face the nearest tree trunk. Taking the knife carefully in his right hand, he carved an arrow pointing back toward the farm.

He closed up the rucksack, clasping it tight and swinging it over his back, along with the rifle. His eyesight seemed slightly better and he could now make out some of the shapes of the stones and grass at his feet. He adjusted the gun on his shoulders before slowly walking deeper into the dark trees.

What was he looking for exactly? Movement, for one. Or anything else that could indicate the presence of another being. Hopefully, the first living thing he came across would be his father. He didn't want to consider the alternative. Levi's gaze moved continuously, sweeping the ground, then to the left and to the right. Every few minutes he would carve another arrow into the bark of a tree. It became almost ritualistic. Look down, look left, look right, carve. Look down, look left, look right, carve.

Within several minutes, the boy became familiar with the overall feel of the woods. It was simply different combinations of the same thing: trees, moss, dirt, rocks, leaves. He saw a few broken branches here and there, indicating something had come through. But it was just as likely a wild animal as it was his father since the path wasn't the width or height he'd expect for a human. He saw some torn up dirt, some weeds mixed in with the long strands of grass. But then–

"Wait," Levi breathed aloud.

He stared at a stretch of mud on the ground, a few feet in front of him. Upon walking closer, he saw there were some prints, pressed into the mud. He squinted at them for a moment, but once he was certain he wouldn't get any further without additional light, he pulled off his rucksack and rummaged inside for the box of matches.

Levi struck the match and crouched down, careful not to step on any of the prints. At first, they looked like they came from some sort of dog. But dogs didn't normally travel this far from town, not even strays. There was no food for them out here, they had a much higher likelihood of finding dinner somewhere in town. From that deduction, he determined it was probably a coyote.

As he followed the path with his eyes, though, he realized there was another set of tracks there. More round and circular, almost like a hoof. It was layered over two or three of the coyote prints, then became the only print in sight. No – not quite layered. Two of the prints had a front half with rounded toes like a dog or a coyote, but the back half was circular. He swept the lit match from the left to the right, confirming his findings. He wasn't mistaken – the tracks started off as coyote and ended with something looking like a horse or cow. Levi kept his eyes on the finding, like staring at the mysterious tracks would magically give him the answers he needed. The pieces were there, right in front of him. He just couldn't make sense of it. Was the creature part animal, part human? Or part *two* animals, part human? But what–

A branch snapped. Levi leapt to his feet and swung the rifle off his shoulder, dropping the match in the process. It was instantly snuffed out in the mud at his feet. Once again plunged into darkness, the boy raised the gun where he thought the noise had come from: directly behind him. He squinted, straining his eyes in the dim light for any sign of movement

There was another crack, closer this time. Levi almost took a step back, but remembered the precious evidence behind him and forced himself to hold his ground. He opened his eyes as wide as he could, praying that the little adjustment his eyes had made would prove enough to determine friend from foe.

A crinkle of leaves, the scrape of a stone. This was the stride length and pace of a human. A human was stepping toward him.

Levi pursed his lips and steeled the weapon in his hands. "Who's there?" he half-whispered, half-shouted. "Pa, is that you?"

A moment of silence.

"Levi?"

The boy heaved a sigh and let the gun fall to his side. "Austin, what in Christ's name are you doin' here?"

A shadowed figure stepped into the clearing. His face moved into a patch of moonlight and Levi could confirm it was, in fact, his brother.

"I – I'm sorry," Austin said, his hands fidgeting with the fringe of his shirt. He couldn't look Levi in the eyes. "I know you told me to stay, and I wanted to, but – well, I know you're lookin' out for Pa and tryin' to keep him safe, but I thought to myself, who's gonna look out for *you* and watch your back while you're lookin' for Pa? And I know you told me someone needs to watch the farm, but I talked to Glenn and he said if somethin' happened to all three of us, he and his Pa would take care of our herd and make sure they were alright." He paused to catch his breath and met Levi's disapproving gaze with one of imploring. "And the more I thought about it, the more I figured... this is my farm and my home just the same as it's yours and Pa's. It's my duty to protect it, too. And the best thing I can do is to be out here, helpin' you. So – so I need to be here."

Austin straightened his shoulders and placed his hands on his hips to emphasize his point. Levi was quiet for a moment, look-ing over his brother from top to bottom. It was clear the boy had been running. His forehand was damp with sweat, the bottom of his pant legs caked with mud. He had run into the woods with no supplies, no direction. Solely focusing on the hope that he would find his older brother. Levi knew he should be angry with him for disobeying his orders and a part of him was.

But a larger part of him was relieved that his brother was here with him in the darkness. He was only eleven years old and he was willing to risk his life to save his family. What more could you ask from a boy?

Levi pursed his lips, shaking his head like he was think-ing hard. "That was some speech," he mused, then shrugged. "Alright, I guess you can stay."

Austin released a breath, a grin spreading over his face. "Thanks, Le– I mean, I was gonna stay here regardless of what you said. You can't *make* me go back, y'know?"

"Whatever you say." Levi pointed to the ground and revealed his finding. "But lookit this."

Austin stepped closer, peering intently. "What is it?"

Levi struck another match and held it toward the muddy shapes. "Two kinds of tracks, coyote and cow. But it looks like–"

"Like they blend into each other," Austin finished. He pressed a finger into the mud and it came away coated in brown goop. "These are fresh, the mud is still damp."

Levi nodded. "That's why I'm thinkin' it likely wasn't two different animals. Maybe the creature has different front and back paws?"

Austin was quiet, still analyzing the tracks. "Maybe," he said finally. He pointed ahead of the most forward print. "Should we keep followin' them this way?"

"Yeah, but keep an eye out. Whatever it is might be nearby."

The two brothers continued walking in silence. Every few minutes they would hear a rustle and freeze, but it always ended up as an insect or a stray gust of breeze. At least, that's what Levi convinced himself it was. Although the match eventually burned out, the boys kept moving forward in the darkness. The tracks didn't seem to change again from what they could see.

"I think there's somethin' up ahead," whispered Levi, pushing through a few branches and craning his neck. "It looks like… a clearin' of some sort."

The younger brother made a face. "Do you smell that?"

Levi paused and crinkled his nose. "Yeah, I do. Smells like rotten meat."

As he shoved through the last few bushes, the scent only grew more rancid until it seemed to suffocate the air around them. By the time he stumbled into the clearing, Levi's eyes were watering. Austin covered his nose and mouth with his shirt, coughing hoarsely. There was a break in the trees, a small area clear of rocks or bushes. Across from the boys was a mound of something Levi couldn't quite make out in the darkness, but looked like dirt. He heard a buzzing, somewhat insect-like, but louder than any bug he'd ever heard. Levi held his breath and he reached into his bag, pulling out another match. When it lit, he stumbled back as the scene came into view.

It wasn't a mound of dirt across from them. It was a pile of blood, guts, and bones. He saw a perfectly preserved set of ribs on one side and the skull of a cow sticking out from the top. Another skull, of a horse, sat off to the side. It was picked completely clean without a speck of meat on it. The carnage was speckled with black dots that moved and flitted from place to place. Flies. Hundreds of them, flying around and darting between the mounds of tissue.

Austin turned away, retching. "What – what is that?" he choked out.

"Innards, I think," Levi responded, forcing himself to breathe through his mouth, "and bones from animals. Some of it looks old, like the bones have been here a while. But other stuff is fresh." He pointed to what appeared to be a trail of intestines. "That looks new, the blood is still wet."

"You think the creature did that?"

"Maybe but… most animals eat what they kill. If the thing we're lookin' for did this, why'd it leave the meat here to rot?"

Austin swallowed, his voice shaking. "If it ain't eatin' what it kills… why is it killin'?"

Levi said nothing, but in his mind, he was wondering the exact same thing. As they stood there, he could feel the seconds slipping away. They could ponder what it all meant once Pa was found and the creature was dead. But right now, there wasn't time for wondering. He straightened up, saying, "If it comes here often, we gotta find a place to hide. Ambush it when it comes back. Right now, we're out in the open."

Austin nodded and started to step back into the denser trees, but paused. "You hear that?"

"Hear wh…" Levi began, but he *did* hear something. A rustling of leaves, a collection of whispers. Multiple voices. "Austin," whispered Levi suddenly. "How'd you find me so quick?"

"I walked into the woods and saw the match."

Both brothers looked wide-eyed at the lit match still clutched in Levi's hand. He instantly dropped it to the ground, pressing his boot into it and shoving it into the muddy soil.

But it was too late.

"Hey, you sons o' bitches," called a voice. "We know you're there."

Austin instantly stepped behind Levi, removing a knife from his pants pocket and snapping it open. Levi raised his gun up toward the sound. The noises grew closer and closer, and Levi could pick out at least two distinct sets of footsteps.

"Cole and Jesse," he called back, forcing his voice to keep steady. "Go back home. You dunno what you're doin'."

Just as Austin had done minutes before, a pair of shadows stepped into the moonlight. Both had triumphant, sneering smiles on their faces. "Oh, I think we do," Cole replied, then paused. He sniffed and curled his lip. "What in Christ's name is that smell?" His eyes stopped on the pile behind the brother. "Jesus – did you do that?"

"No," Levi said quickly. "We found it just now."

Cole rolled his eyes. "Sure you did." He started to step forward, but Levi raised the barrel of the gun. The boy froze and raised his hands. "Whoa, no need for that, now. We just wanna talk."

"Did you *just wanna talk* when you jumped me in the market?"

Cole and Jesse exchanged looks. "That was different," Jesse muttered. His nose was still blackened and swollen.

"Yeah, *very* different," Austin sneered.

Levi threw him a glance that said *let me handle this* and returned his attention to the pair. "Listen, I don't care what anyone thinks. We're not doin' any of this, we've been tryin' to stop it. There's some sorta creature in these woods, killin' animals and people. It's the same thing that killed my cow, Glenn's dog – and probably my Ma."

Jesse narrowed his eyes. "I thought your Ma got poisoned."

"So did I. But my Pa lied to us. He lied to the whole town and we're just realizin' now." Levi paused for a moment to gather his thoughts. "I don't got time to explain. But it wasn't my brother and me who did these killin's. There's… somethin' else in these woods. Somethin' not natural."

"The hell you mean by that?" spat Cole.

Levi tilted his head, gesturing to the mound of gore. "We followed some animal tracks we saw and found this. The tracks were strange, I couldn't recognize them. An animal normally eats what it kills, but whatever this thing is ain't normal." Hedging a bet, Levi aimed the weapon toward the ground and held up his opposite hand in a sign of peace. "Listen, I'll explain everythin' I know. But first, you and your brother have to promise not to try anythin' stupid. We need you on our side if we're gonna beat this thing."

Cole's eyes flicked from Levi's face to the barrel of the gun, then back up. "It ain't us you have to convince."

Before Levi could process his words, he heard footsteps running up behind him. One hand grabbed the rifle and another shoved the square of his back. The weapon was torn from his grasp as he tumbled to the ground. The impact knocked the wind out of him, but he had the strength to flip over onto his back while he caught his breath.

The gun was pointing directly between his eyes. Keeping his head still, Levi flicked his gaze upward to identify the assailant. "Amos," he breathed.

Jed's brother wore a blank expression on his face. He didn't seem to register the fact that one twitch of his finger would end Levi's life. He simply stood there, weapon in hand. Even in the dim light, Levi could see the hollowness of his eyes and the matting of his hair.

The boy was out of his mind.

"Amos, please." Levi's voice broke. He craned his neck

backward, away from the muzzle, but Amos leaned forward to follow him. "We're not murderers, we would never do somethin' like that."

Amos blinked. "Sure you wouldn't."

Levi closed his eyes, silently praying. "Believe me, I am so sorry about Jed. I wish it never happened."

Levi's head was pressed into the ground now. With nowhere else to go, he tensed as the tip of the gun touched his forehead. Amos looked at the pile of bones and innards, then back to the boy. "You're only sorry you got caught," he said.

Levi heard the safety click off. The air froze in his chest and he steeled himself for the pain. His mind flashed with memories of hugging his mother, laughing with his brother, his father glaring down at him in disdain. Would that really be the last moment he spent with his Pa? An overwhelming wave of regret and helplessness washed over him. There was nothing he could do now but wait for the loud bang, the flash of agony, and the darkness.

Instead, he heard a wet thud.

Levi's eyes shot open. Austin was standing next to Amos, the hilt of a knife still clutched in his hand. The blade was buried deep in Amos' right shoulder.

Austin stepped back, mouth ajar, staring at what he had just done.

Amos cocked his head to look at the knife. He removed his left hand from the gun and grabbed the metal sticking out of his arm. He winced ever so slightly as the blade slid out, dripping dark blood. He blinked at it, observing the droplets falling onto the dirt below. Then, he let it fall out of his hand. His gaze slowly lifted to look at Levi's brother. "You shouldn't have done that," he said.

Amos aimed the rifle at Austin and fired.

Chapter Ten

A SCREAM RIPPED ITSELF from Levi's lungs as he threw himself toward Amos. He wrapped himself around the boy's legs and pulled him down with all his strength.

As Amos lost his balance and began to fall, Levi looked back toward his brother. Austin had collapsed. Levi couldn't see much, but from what he could see, his chest was splattered with blood.

For a moment, Levi's eyes burned with the memory of his father carrying his mother home. Painted red.

Amos collapsed into the mud, instinctively putting his arms out behind him to break his fall. When he did so, he let go of the rifle. It followed him down, landing on his ribs.

Levi wasn't in control of his next movements. One second he was sprawled in the mud, arms still tightly wrapped around the boy's calves. The next, he was on top of Amos. He shoved the gun to the side with one hand, then used his other arm to twist the boy onto his side. Amos didn't have time to react as Levi hooked the crook of his arm around the boy's neck. With the other arm, he wrapped around his fist and pulled upward.

On a normal day, Amos could've easily thrown Levi off or at least twisted back over to break his grip. But at that moment, something inside Levi had snapped. The aggression and ruthlessness he felt was almost instinctual, a long-repressed impulse that had been forced to resurface when he saw his brother collapse to the ground.

Amos struggled with all his might, throwing his elbows back into Levi's chest and flailing his feet. In the back of his mind, Levi knew he should be hurting. But his mind was only focused on squeezing. Squeezing until the boy stopped moving.

Suddenly, Levi felt more hands on him. Cole and Jesse each grabbed one of Levi's arms and slowly pried him off of the boy. Once released, Amos collapsed onto all fours, coughing and heaving.

The boys dragged Levi away about a yard away before tossing him into the mud. Levi still felt his heart pounding in his chest, but something about the boys interrupting his tirade had brought his mind back into his body.

Levi's gaze snapped to his brother, lying motionless on the ground.

"Austin," he gasped, standing and stumbling toward him. He knelt beside him, lifting up his brother's soaking shirt and searching for the entrance wound. Austin's front was a mess of blood and it took him a moment to find it. When he finally did, he breathed a sigh of relief. It was an inch next to his right arm, in the meat of his chest. It still looked bad, but it could've been much worse. A few inches to the left and down and it would've blown right threw his heart.

Levi pulled his own shirt off and ripped it in half, tying it around his brother's wound. It wasn't perfect, but it was all he could think of to slow the blood flow.

Levi put two fingers to his brother's neck. It was faint, but there was a heartbeat. "Aus," Levi whispered, forcing the words past the tightness in his throat. "Aus, please, wake up."

After the longest second of Levi's life, Austin's eyes slowly blinked open. "Levi," he whimpered. "It… hurts."

"I know." Levi saw the piece of his shirt growing dark on Austin's chest and quickly undid the knot. As he started retying it, he whispered, "I'm sorry. We'll get you outta here." He pulled the knot taut and Austin gritted his teeth. "I'm so – so sorry, but please, Aus, you gotta get up."

While Levi continued coaxing his brother, he heard the voices of Cole and Jesse behind him.

"W-what do we do now?"

"I didn't know he was gonna try 'n kill him."

"Neither did I. This wasn't what we said we were gonna do."

"Do you think we should get the sheriff?"

"Not unless you want to spend the rest of your life in jail."

The group froze when another bullet clicked into the chamber of the rifle. Levi turned away from his brother to stare into Amos' eyes. He was standing now, shakily, holding the weapon up once again. "I–" he coughed for a moment, struggling to clear his throat. He rasped, "I'm not leavin' 'til they're both dead."

Levi understood now. There was no reasoning with this boy. No amount of begging or pleading was going to change his mind. The only thing that would appease him was vengeance. Levi glanced toward Cole and Jesse, hoping that they would see what was going on, that they would put a stop to the madness. But they were frozen in place, staring wide-eyed at the weapon in Amos' hands.

Behind Amos, something caught Levi's attention. Two eyes were peering out from the trees, watching the scene unfold. Not a human this time – an animal. The head of a cow.

At first, Levi thought his mind had to be playing tricks on him. There were no cows this deep in the woods, and certainly none that would be attracted to the sound of a gunshot. But when Amos saw the look in his eyes and turned to stare too, Levi realized he could see it, too. "What the…" Amos muttered, aiming the gun toward the animal.

A crinkle of leaves and the cow disappeared into the darkness. The boys stared at the spot it had just been as Levi's mind whirred.

It finally clicked.

"Austin," he whispered. "We need to r–"

A shadow burst through the trees, bounding straight toward Cole and Jesse. The two were caught by surprise and thrown to the ground. The moonlight only allowed Levi to see glimpses of the creature as it pawed at Jesse's chest and face. The beast was at least the size of a horse, but much wider and covered in fur.

A bear.

Jesse's scream was gut-wrenching, but Levi tried his hardest to ignore it while he wrapped his arms around his brother's chest. "No time," he hissed frantically to Austin. "We need to leave. Right now."

Austin gasped in pain, clutching his chest with his left hand. Levi forced himself under his brother's good arm. Austin tried to step forward and immediately fell to his knees.

"C'mon." Levi wrapped his arms around his limp brother, shoving upward with all his strength to bring him back to his feet.

Austin's head lolled to one side, his eyes half-closed. "I can't see," he muttered. "It's all black."

"It's alright," Levi whispered hurriedly, a terrible crunching noise from behind sending a wave of nausea coursing through him. "You're fine, we'll rest in a bit. But I need you to get up, Aus. *Get up.*"

The urgency in his brother's voice seemed to snap Austin into a more lucid state. He rose and leaned into Levi's chest. The boys began to shakily step forward at a pace that was interminable to Levi. At any moment he expected to hear a rush of footsteps behind them, feel the hot, acrid breath of the animal sweep across their back.

The pair jumped when a gunshot rang out. Levi glanced over his shoulder to see Amos aiming the gun at the bear.

A dark spot bloomed from the bear's chest from where it was struck, but it hardly seemed to notice. It snarled at Amos and the boy stumbled back a few steps, fumbling to reload the gun. Cole was standing beside him, wide eyes locked on his brother. The beast looked up, its mouth awash in red. Only Jesse's feet were visible from where Levi and his brother were standing. A maroon puddle crept along the grass, spreading outward from the boy's body.

Even as the bear lunged forward, Cole never took his eyes off his brother. At the last minute, he tried to stumble out of reach, but it wasn't enough. The boy let out a scream when its claws tore through his shirt, into his back. His fingers grabbed at the dirt, desperately trying to pull himself away.

Levi tore his gaze away from the carnage, twisted back around and forced himself forward. "Don't look back," he whispered to his brother. "One step at a time. Left–"

Another gunshot sounded and the bear let out a guttural sound that made Levi's legs go weak. He gripped his brother tighter, willing the pair to step further, to move faster. "Lean on me, we've got to keep movin'. C'mon, Aus, I've got you."

The more steps they took, the more dulled the sounds of the commotion became. Eventually, Levi picked up the pace to a light jog. Every few seconds, he glanced behind them. But for the time being, it didn't seem like they were being followed.

Not long after, Austin went limp in Levi's arms. The older

brother couldn't shift the dead weight in time and the pair collapsed to the ground.

"I – I'm sorry, Levi," Austin murmured. His lips were pale, his eyes hazy and bloodshot. "I just – I can't."

"It's alright," Levi replied quickly, glancing around. If they couldn't go any further at the moment, they at least needed cover while Austin regained his strength and they figured out what to do next. "There. Just a little further, get behind that log. We'll stay there until–"

Another gunshot. Levi pulled his brother to his feet. The pair stumbled a few steps more until they knelt behind the downed tree, although it was more of a semi-controlled fall.

Just as they crouched into the shadows, a person burst into the clearing. Levi peaked his head just far enough upward to make out the figure of Amos. He was still clutching the gun, but now he was covered in streaks of mud and blood. His brow was damp with perspiration and he hastily wiped sweat out of his eyes with one hand.

The boy was adjusting the weapon in his hands when it struck.

Levi ducked down, covering his mouth with one hand to silence his breathing. It had come out of nowhere – no bear could move that quietly. It looked smaller now, much smaller. Almost like it was an entirely different animal.

Levi couldn't help himself. He had to look. He met Austin's gaze. Even in the boy's woozy state, he wanted to know the truth, too. The older brother slowly raised a finger to his lips.

Together, the boys raised their heads to peek over the log.

There was a dog standing over Amos' body. It had a brown head with long fur, drenched in red, with patches of black and white on its body. A skirt of mismatched cloth was tied around its middle. From what Levi could see, it had dealt a deadly blow to Amos' neck. The boy wasn't moving anymore, but the pool of blood still grew on the forest floor.

As the boys stared, however, the scene began to change.

The animal's fur retreated into its skin. It lifted itself off of its front paws so it was standing upright. The bones of its legs stretched out, increasing in length. The skirt moved with it, shifting upwards and swaying in the moonlight. No, not a skirt. Chain. A chain of pelts in all different shapes and sizes was now wrapped around the torso of the bipedal figure. Its head grew and rounded its edges, like the very bones themselves were shifting beneath its skin.

Within a matter of seconds, where once had stood a dog was a man. He was tall, muscular, wearing nothing aside from the pelts that hung from his waist. His back was to the boys as he inspected the body.

"Change," murmured Levi.

Austin looked at him. "What?"

"It changes." Levi's eyes widened, unable to stop staring. "That's what Pa wrote in his diary, right? He watched it *change*."

"You don't mean…"

"It can change what it looks like."

The man suddenly bent down over Amos. He held up one hand and his fingers began sprouting dark, coarse hair. The fingernails lengthened and sharpened until a claw was attached to the end of the human arm.

The talons came down, moving across Amos' chest. Levi and Austin both craned their necks to see what the creature was doing, but its back was still turned to them. The man let out a hiss, then plunged the arm downward. It struggled for a moment and lifted up something clenched in its fist victoriously.

Levi swallowed down bile as he stared at the human heart clutched in the creature's hand.

The organ shuddered and throbbed, the nerves threaded through it pulsing with the dwindling energy of its former host. The man stared at it and slowly brought it to his face. He opened his mouth, revealing teeth much too sharp for a human. It took a bite, tearing easily through the dense muscle and layered tissue. Syrupy blood dripped from the corners of his mouth, running down his chin and neck. It was only at this point that it turned far enough in the direction of the boys that they could recognize the creature's face.

Both boys started, tensing from their hidden position. Levi had enough self-control to bite back the cry that threatened to break forth, but Austin was not as refined.

"Pa?" he whispered.

The man instantly whipped its head in their direction. The two boys ducked down. Much as every cell in his body screamed at him to run, Levi stayed frozen. He twisted his head around to stare through a thin sliver in the log's exterior to stare at the man he once knew.

Its face looked like Pa, it was the same size as Pa – if Levi hadn't just seen him change, he never would've known the difference. Was it possible it *was* their father?

Change. The creature could change into different animals – and different humans, too. That dog and bear were proof. But how? Is that why it looked like Pa? And what did he just do to Amos?

All of these thoughts flashed through his mind in a fraction of a second. In that time, the man changed again. He shrunk, his hair grew lighter, his muscles less toned. Still human, but smaller now. Younger, and familiar.

"Levi?" the thing that looked like Amos called. *"Austin? Is that you?"*

The brothers met each other's eyes when it all came together.

The thing in front of them wasn't Amos. It wasn't Pa, either. Levi recognized most of the animals on the skirt – a cow's skin, a fox's, and a dog's. Not just any dog's; a Collie's.

"Ryder," breathed Levi.

Austin's breath hitched in his chest. "It can change into the things it kills."

Levi nodded frantically, not daring to speak another word as the pieces fell into place. Once the thing killed another being, it had the ability to transform. For animals, it seemed like it had to take its fur and hold its pelt to gain its form. That's what the mound of innards was from, it was the leftovers. For humans, it needed to consume...

Levi stared at Austin, weighing his odds as the footsteps of the thing approached. His brother's breathing was shallow, his gaze unfocused. There was no way he would be able to keep up.

Decision made, Levi reached inside his pocket and retrieved the compass. He grabbed both of Austin's hands and closed them around the round metal. "I'm gonna start runnin'," he whispered frantically. "When I do, count to thirty and start runnin' east. Use the compass. It'll take you home. Look for the arrows on the trees when you get closer. Do not follow me – I'll try to lead it away as far as I can before headin' toward the farm. Do you understand?"

Austin nodded, mouth pursed and eyes wet with tears. The younger pulled his older brother towards him in a damp, metallic-scented embrace.

Levi wished he could stay like that for longer, but he forced himself to pull away. "Thirty seconds," he repeated. Then, he took off.

Right as Levi took his first step, he heard the pounding of footfalls behind him. It started off as the clunky steps of a human, but soon changed into something lighter, more dexterous. He glanced over his shoulder and saw a flash of red dart among the green underbrush.

A fox.

Before Levi had handed off the compass to his brother, he had glanced at it himself to know his orientation. The direction he was currently running in now was northeast. He needed to stay on this path for a few minutes, then he would start arching toward the house. Hopefully, he would run far enough that when he finally headed toward home, Austin was already there and safe with Glenn.

As he ran, his actions were frenzied but for once his mind was calm. He had just watched two people die, Jesse and Amos. And Cole was probably dead, too. He had never seen someone die in front of him – he was pretty sure Ma was already dead when his father had brought her back to the house.

And if the way the creature turned into Amos was true for all humans it killed, then that meant Pa…

Levi stumbled for a moment, catching himself and taking off again at a sprint. There was no time to dwell on it now. If Pa was gone, he was gone. Now Levi's duty was to save what was left of his family.

He would mourn later.

Maybe it was the adrenaline or the horror at just having watched his classmates die, but Levi was able to weave through the woods expertly at a pace he didn't even know he was capable of. Though he was barely able to differentiate the shapes and shadows around him, he somehow correctly placed each step he made to avoid tripping.

After a few minutes, he threw another glance behind him.

He didn't see the creature, animal or human, pursuing him any longer. That didn't mean it wasn't still close by, though. Watching.

Levi prayed that enough time had passed between him running and Austin setting off, and began to gradually turn toward what he thought was close to east. He hoped his estimations were accurate enough to land him at the base of the hill that led to the farm. Too little angle and he would end up at the edge of the forest amongst the uncultivated land beyond the farm grounds. Too much and he would never reach a break in the trees and would simply keep running until his legs failed him.

Disturbingly, the second seemed to be a more likely possibility as time went on. Something about taking that final turn toward the farm made Levi's limbs feel like they weighed much more than they had seconds before. His breathing became shallow and his chest burned, but he continued pushing himself forward. He was in the homeward stretch now. And Lord knew Austin couldn't protect himself in the current state he was in.

Levi wasn't sure how long he ran for. It felt interminable. Every few moments, he glanced behind him. The hair on his arms was constantly raised, his mind stifled by the feeling of being watched. But no matter how many times he scanned the forest around him, he couldn't see any sign of the creature. Or his brother.

It both gave him comfort and made his stomach twist in fear.

Levi felt himself slowing down. He kept trying to push his lungs to breathe deeper, shove his legs to pump faster, but the adrenaline had run its course. His thoughts started to spin wildly, heart pounding in his chest. He should've reached it by now, he must've overshot – should he just make a sharp left and hope for the best? But if he reached the end of the forest, what if he couldn't see the farm? He might run off in the wrong direction, not knowing which direction was home. He couldn't leave Austin that long, who knew how long he–

"Yes!" Levi almost collapsed when he saw the marking on the tree. One of his arrows, pointing to the left. He was correct, he had overshot the angle a bit. Thank God he saw it, otherwise who knew how much longer he'd have been running.

Rejuvenated, Levi took off in the direction the arrow pointed. He staggered through the mismatched trees and shoved his hands through branches. He passed two more arrows as he continued forward until finally he saw a break in the trees. With both hands, he pushed himself through the last few feet of bushes and staggered into the open air.

Levi inhaled deeply, breathing comfortably for the first time since he entered the forest. He only allowed himself a few seconds of relief before turning around and looking between the trunks.

Still nothing, but this wasn't entirely a cause for celebration. While the creature was no longer in sight, neither was Austin.

The boy took a moment to catch his breath, then sprinted up the hill in the direction of home. Although the situation was dire, it was still a crushing relief to be once more surrounded by familiar sights. Levi passed the edge of the fence, then the barn, then the chicken coop, and finally reached the house. When he didn't see Glenn sitting outside, he ran up the front steps and banged his fist on the front door.

"Glenn!" he called. "Austin! Are you alright?"

Levi waited with baited breath until he heard a lock turn from inside. The door opened a crack, just enough for an eye to peek out.

"Oh, Levi," Glenn breathed, swinging open the door and ushering the boy inside. "I saw Amos, Cole, and Jesse follow Austin. They were headed for the farm, but once they saw Aus runnin' to the woods, they turned and went for him instead. I tried to warn him, but I don't think he heard me call his name. Did he find you?"

Levi's heart sank. "Wait… is Austin not here?"

A glint of panic entered Glenn's expression. "No, should he be? I've been keepin' an eye out, but I haven't seen anythin' besides you since the three boys left."

"Glenn, Austin is in trouble. We saw the creature, it–" Levi's mouth went dry and he couldn't complete the sentence. He swallowed past the lump in his throat and continued, "Austin got shot. I sent him ahead of me and tried to lead it away myself, he shoulda made it back here by now. I need you to find the sheriff and bring him here." Levi crossed to the other side of the room and removed the last Remington from the wall. "We're gonna need all the help we can get to kill this thing."

"What is it? Is it a bear?"

Levi thought for a second, then shook his head. "It's too complicated, I'll explain when you get back. All you need to know is Austin is in danger and we need to kill it before it kills him." He motioned Glenn toward the door as he loaded the revolver. "Go, now. There's no time."

Glenn relented at first, but turned back to the boy as he reached the door. "What about the farm? Who's gonna protect it from the boys?"

Levi froze. "They're dead, Glenn," he murmured. "Amos, Cole, Jesse – it killed all of 'em."

Glenn's eyes widened. "What about your Pa?" When Levi shook his head, he released a breath. "Christ. I – I'll get the sheriff." He looked at his friend for a long moment. "Levi, I… I'm so sorry."

Levi didn't know how to respond, so he just nodded. As

Glenn took off down the hill, Levi dropped his bag to the floor, removed his knife and shoved it into his back pocket. He took a moment to wipe at his eyes before confirming the gun was loaded properly.

Six bullets. He prayed it would be enough to hold it off until Glenn returned.

Chapter Eleven

L EVI REMEMBERED TO take one more item with him as he left. An oil lamp. Although the creature may be able to see at night in certain forms, he wasn't about to give it the upper hand if he could avoid it.

As Levi stepped outside, he noticed something strange. The night was completely silent. All of the animals were huddled inside the barn. The crickets refused to sing. There wasn't even a breeze. It was as if the very air itself could sense that something was coming.

Or it knew that something was already here.

Levi strode up the hill and down the other side. There was a large stretch of flat land at the bottom of the hill in front of the treeline. He prayed Austin would be there, waiting for him and he could get him home before taking care of the creature.

As Levi approached the bottom of the hill, he saw something emerge from the trees.

"Austin!" he gasped in relief, but stopped.

The figure was too tall, too muscular. Levi lit the oil lamp and it confirmed his worst fear.

"Pa," whispered Levi, shakily setting down the lantern. Even in the dim, flickering light, there was no mistaking the man. His face was blank, disturbingly expressionless and his steps were calculated.

This wasn't his father. It wasn't even human.

"You're not Pa," Levi said, partially talking to the creature and partially in an attempt to convince himself. The boy pulled the gun from its holster, facing the barrel toward the thing that looked like his father. He steeled his breath and shouted, "Where's my brother?!"

It walked forward with slow, methodical steps. Levi mirrored it, taking a step back every time it moved closer.

"I know you can speak, you son of a bitch," he shouted. He spared a glance over his shoulder, praying Glenn would hurry back. When he looked forward, his father was smiling now. It still didn't say a word.

Levi gritted his teeth, raised his gun. "Please change," he muttered to himself. "Please, please change. Don't make me shoot—"

As if it was acting out of mercy, Pa crouched down. Levi saw dark fur sprout from its skin. Its arms and legs thickened as its back arched upward. It placed its hands on the dusty ground to stand on all fours. Moments later, a bear stared back at him with beady, hungry eyes.

Although Levi could breathe easier now that he wasn't looking at Pa, it didn't last long. Mentally, it would be an easier task to kill the creature now, but physically it had just gotten a whole lot harder.

Six bullets. That's all he had to work with.

The bear snarled, foam dripping from its jowls. Then, it charged.

As the animal grew near, Levi felt a wave of calm wash over him, like his mind was separate from his body. His legs tingled with a sudden energy and he instantly knew what to do. Almost as if he had been training for this exact moment.

Seconds before the thing struck, Levi side-stepped out of the way. It skidded to a stop, turned back, and rushed forward again. The boy began to move one way, then threw his body weight in the other, keeping the weapon clutched to his chest. The animal bounded past him, struggling to slow its momentum. Levi lifted the gun while the bear was still off-balance and aimed at its center. He released a breath, steadied his hands, and pulled the trigger.

The kickback of the gun sent Levi staggering back a step, but so did the animal. The bear growled, flicking its snout toward its front right shoulder. Levi had struck it, but it wasn't enough to kill it. The creature returned its attention to Levi and began striding forward once again.

With shaking hands, Levi started to reload. But he felt the weapon fight back. It was jammed. The boy's eyes widened as the bear pounded toward him, realizing there wasn't enough time to run. On instinct, he lifted the gun to cover his head just when the creature reached him. The two fell to the ground, the bear's paws landing on either side of Levi's head. It shifted its weight to its left side, lifting up its right claw to strike. Keeping the revolver raised with one hand, Levi fumbled for his knife with the other. Just as the bear's paw came down, he slid the knife from his pocket and jammed it into the animal's eye.

Levi felt a ribbon of pain race across his left arm. The bear let out a shriek, stumbling backward, and Levi rolled a few feet away. He hissed and quickly glanced at his left arm. It was shredded, trails of blood streaming down his arm and through his shirt. But just like it had in the forest, the adrenaline pushed him forward and dulled his pain. He worked quickly, gingerly holding the gun with his left hand and prying out the jammed bullet with his right. As he did, he glanced up. The thing was pawing at its eye, probably doing more damage than good by twisting the knife. It only took a few seconds for it to pry the knife free, though, and it fell to the ground moments later.

Levi was running out of time.

As he looked back down at the gun, he heard its heavy footfalls against the ground. Levi pried out the jammed bullet and threw it to the side. He looked up. It was no more than a few yards away, he didn't have a second to spare.

Levi raised the gun and fired. The bear let out a cry. It was mere feet away now, bounding toward him with incredible speed. The shell flew out when he reloaded, stepping backward as fast as he could without losing balance. He knew this was his last chance. Any longer and it would be too late.

The boy averted his eyes, lifted the gun toward the sound of impending death, and pulled the trigger.

A bang, a smatter of footfalls.

Then, silence.

Levi kept his eyes shut, hardly daring to believe he was safe. When he did open his eyes, he saw the bear had collapsed midstride. Levi stared at it, afraid to blink, waiting for it to jump up and attack once again. It didn't move. At least, not at first. But as he watched, it seemed like the creature began to shrink in on itself, fur curling inward and revealing brown flesh. The muscular paws of the bear separated into five fingers. The skirt of pelts shrunk with the host, wrapping itself around the man's torso. Even though the person was lying face down, Levi recognized the shape and size of him instantly.

Pa lay before him, blood leaking from a bullet hole in the back of his head.

The cry that had been building up in Levi's chest since the

night first began burst forth as he knelt beside the body of his father. He knew this really wasn't his father – his actual body was somewhere deep in the woods, disemboweled by the thing he had just killed. But in this moment, it was all he had to mourn over. His father's right shoulder was a mess of dark blood, as were two other exit wounds on his legs. Levi longed to see his father's face, but he didn't dare turn the body over. He couldn't stand to see such a head wound inflicted on the man who raised him.

Levi dropped his head, laying a hand on Pa's bloodied and stolen form. He wanted to say something, to honor his father and his legacy. But no words came. His throat closed, hot tears falling onto the man's back. He had forced himself to be strong for so long, but his willpower had finally broken.

The only thought that brought him peace was knowing his father was now reunited with Eloise – and Levi had slaughtered the thing that had made him and his brother orphans.

Levi longed to stay in that moment, to let every emotion drown him until only numbness remained. But the thought of Austin being lost and alone in the woods calmed his mind. As he wiped his eyes with the back of his good hand, a wave of nauseating pain rolled over him. He looked again at his arm, which was now fully coated in red. It burned and throbbed with every movement he made, the cloth of his shirt pulling along his raw skin. He looked around the ground for his knife and found it among a patch of nearby grass. He wiped the back and front on his pants leg, then straightened out his left arm and began to cut away the layers of flannel with the knife. Once it was freed, he grit his teeth and slowly peeled away the cloth from the wound. Some of it came away easily, other parts stung like needles. He forced himself to breathe deeply and keep going, even when his right hand began to shake with exertion. Finally, the last piece was removed. He tensed as he turned his arm over, inspecting the damage.

The cuts were deeper than he thought; when he moved his hand, he could see the muscles in his arm flex and contract. The wound felt oddly cold. Nothing seemed damaged, though. He could still move his fingers and twist his wrist, though the twisting motion sent a spiral of excruciating agony through his forearm.

"Probably not good," he muttered to himself as the pain subsided. He considered tying a tourniquet, but decided to wait until Glenn got there. It would be hard enough to do it with one hand and his friend should be returning any moment with the sheriff. He let his left arm hang limply at his side and used his right to gather the gun from where he left it on the ground.

If Austin was smart – and Levi prayed that he was – he would've realized that he couldn't make it back to the farm with his injury and had hidden himself somewhere in the woods. He would have to go west, call his name, and hope his brother would believe it was him and not the creature. But just as Levi was steeling himself to pick up the lantern, something caught his attention.

There were two eyes peering out from the forest.

Levi stepped forward. With the creature and the three boys dead, there was no one else he had to fear.

"Austin?" Levi called out. "Is that you? I killed it, we're safe now."

There was a few seconds pause before a small figure emerged from the treeline.

Levi gasped in relief. "Aus, thank God. Are you alright?" He started to run, but when his brother came into view, he slowed to a stop. It was his brother walking toward him, but something was off. "Where's your shirt?" he asked, but that wasn't it. His gaze drifted to the boy's chest.

The bullet wound wasn't there. His shoulder was completely healed. No scar, no blood. Nothing. Like it never happened.

"Aus?" Levi whispered.

Austin said nothing. Levi's mind reached a conclusion, but his heart rebelled. He blinked his eyes, frantically wanting his brother to reappear the way he had been only minutes prior. But much as he tried to wake himself up from the nightmare, reality stared him down with dead eyes.

This wasn't Austin.

"Oh no," Levi gasped, his throat tightening. "No, please, no."

Austin kept advancing, step by step. Although his expression was completely neutral, when he opened his mouth, the voice that came out was wrought with agony. Like he was being tortured. Like Levi's brother was being secretly killed just out of reach. *"Levi!"* Austin's voice screamed. *"Help me, please!"*

"Stop it!" Levi clamped his hands over his ears, desperate to drown out the sound. "You're not Austin, *you're not Austin!"*

"Levi, make it stop. It hurts so much, do somethin'!"

"Aus," his brother sobbed, stumbling backward, away from the thing wearing his brother's skin. He couldn't think, couldn't walk. His mind rang with the sounds of his brother's anguish. "I'm sorry. I'm so, so sorry."

"Please, Levi, it's killin' me. It's killin' me!"

"He's already dead!" Levi dropped to his knees, his body shaking with sobs. "You're not my brother!"

There were two. There were *two* this whole time. This creature was smarter than its partner, it had watched him. And it knew that Levi found it much easier to kill a faceless animal than a family member.

Levi looked up and found Austin standing over him. He felt his shoulders shaking, knew he was crying, couldn't stop.

Every word that left his brother's lips was a knife to his heart. He grabbed the revolver from beneath him, forced himself to raise it. His left arm screamed as he pointed it between his brother's eyes.

Austin was quiet now, his face as still as stone. Ever so slowly, he leaned forward, bending at the waist. He lowered himself until his forehead lightly pressed against the muzzle of the gun. Austin's pale lips curled into a smile.

"What's wrong, Levi?" the thing whimpered. *"Why won't you help me?"*

"Stop it!" The gun dipped down, but Levi forced it back up. "Stop it, please!"

Austin laughed.

Levi closed his eyes.

His finger tightened around the trigger.

Glenn gasped for air as the Oakley's house came into view. He still clutched the Remington that Levi had given him earlier. His palms were slick with sweat and he fumbled the weapon, but quickly recovered and gripped it tighter.

Once Levi had told Glenn what to do, the boy raced to the sheriff's home and banged on his front door. A flickering light appeared in the window and a bleary-eyed Williams stepped outside. Glenn had frantically explained what Levi told him and where the sheriff needed to go – and that Austin was in danger. The sheriff gave him a strange look and told him to wait while he got changed and prepared his weapon, but Glenn had taken off as soon as the man shut the door. He didn't want to waste a moment where Levi might be fighting this thing on his own. A few minutes later, he was back on the Oakley's farm, praying with every passing second that he wasn't too late.

Glenn raced along the edge of the fence and up the last hill, heading toward the pointed edges of the trees. His legs and lungs burned, but the thought of the Oakley brothers in danger kept him moving. As he reached the crest, he saw the flicker of an oil lantern at the base of the hill.

There was someone standing stock still, facing the forest. Two dark shapes laid on the ground beside them, unmoving.

"Levi!" Glenn called, skidding down the slope. "Levi, is that you? Did–" He stumbled to a stop as the scene came into view. "Christ Almighty…"

Neither of the two figures on the ground were a mysterious, unknown creature like he had expected. They were both *human*. One was a tall man, lying face down in the grass. He was naked aside from a fur skirt tied around his waist. The back of his head was a mess of hair and gore. The other shape was a boy, lying face up, also with fur around his midsection. At first, Glenn could hardly identify him from the amount of blood painting his torso and face. But when the realization hit him, the boy dropped to his knees. "No," he gasped, placing a finger to the boy's neck. He felt warm flesh, but no heartbeat. His gaze shifted back to the man on the ground, breath catching in his throat. He blinked away tears and turned to stare at the standing figure. "What did you do?"

The person slowly turned to face him. His eyes were glassy, face marred with streaks of dirt and blood. "They're dead," Levi muttered. Both of his hands curled around the revolver, twitching and shifting its weight in his hands. "We were wrong. There were two creatures, not one. I killed 'em both."

Glenn stood, the back of one hand pressed against his mouth.

The gun trembled in his grasp. "These aren't creatures," he choked out. "Did – did you do this?"

Levi's head was heavy. It took every ounce of strength for him to move the words past his lips. "They can change. They ain't really Austin and Pa, they just look like 'em."

Glenn took a step back. He slowly wrapped both hands around the weapon. "It was you," he murmured. "It was you this whole time. You *were* the one killin' those people, those animals. You were lyin' to me."

"No." Levi blinked, struggling against the haziness clouding his mind. "It ain't really them… I didn't…"

"Tell me you didn't do this," Glenn said shakily. When Levi didn't reply, he trained the gun on his friend. *"Tell me!"*

The boy stared wearily at the gaping mouth of the Remington, then moved his gaze to meet Glenn's. He wanted to explain to him, wanted to make him understand. But his eyes kept moving to the blood of his brother coating his hands. He smelled the tinge of metal in the air. His mind played back the vision of Austin's eyes dimming as Levi held his stolen body. How his lips formed his older brother's name one last time.

Levi was so, so tired.

Tears streamed down Glenn's face, but his expression remained unyielding. Levi saw his finger twitch on the trigger. But he never pulled it.

Levi almost wished he would.

He couldn't say how long they stayed like that, eyes locked on each other. Eventually, the sound of footsteps echoed down the hill and Sheriff Williams strode into the lamplight. He took in the scene and exchanged a few hushed words with Glenn. A bead of sweat dripped from Glenn's brow as Williams stepped toward Levi.

"Don't try anythin', boy," the sheriff said. Levi simply shut his eyes. He wasn't going to run. Besides, where would he go? He felt his hands tugged behind his back and a rope wrapped around them. The sheriff paused. "We'll deal with your arm later." When Levi didn't respond, Williams pulled the rope tight, cutting into the boy's wrist. But Levi felt no pain.

Once he was secure, the man nudged him forward. The pair walked, Williams keeping one hand pressed between Levi's shoulder blades. Glenn followed closely behind, and when Levi glanced back, he saw Glenn shakily keeping the revolver pointed at his friend. Levi heard him sniffle every so often. He knew he should feel sorrow, should want to explain to Glenn that he didn't do what his friend thought he did. But all he felt was emptiness, a cavernous hole that threatened to swallow him whole if he didn't keep moving.

When they arrived at the jail, the sheriff took the gun from Glenn and gave him an order. The boy took one last, long look at his friend. Levi tried to wordlessly beg for his understanding, that none of this was as it seemed. But after a few seconds, Glenn's eyes sharpened. His expression curdled into something Levi had never seen before. Glenn spat at Levi's feet and left the room. It was in that moment, as Levi watched his last glimpse of hope turn his back on him, that he felt a chill wash over him.

Now, he had no one.

Williams led Levi to a wooden chair and made him sit. Once he secured the boy's bindings to the armrests, he walked out of the room and returned with a roll of gauze. The sheriff unrolled a piece and wrapped it around Levi's bloodied arm hurriedly, the fabric tugging on the boy's wound as he did so. Levi made no sound.

When Williams was satisfied, he pulled up a chair across

from him and asked what had happened that night. But Levi found he couldn't speak. There was a darkness shrouding his vision, invading his mind and muddling his thoughts. Much as he tried to build a sentence and say it aloud, it would crumble too quickly for him to vocalize. Eventually, he closed his mouth and stared at the man.

Levi didn't care what happened to him next. He was pretty sure Williams knew it, too. And although the sheriff kept his expression mostly neutral, the vaguest hint of a smile touched his lips. Williams didn't have to say anything: Levi knew the man now had what he had been looking for.

After several minutes of silence, Williams untied Levi and walked him to a cell. Levi's body ached with exhaustion, but when he laid on the rusty cot, sleep refused to find him. The previous hours played in his mind on repeat. Whenever he got to the point where he looked Austin in the face and pulled the trigger, his mind would instantly go blank and start the night over again. He stayed that way for several hours, tortured by memories, until the first rays began to shine through the square window of the cell. Levi stood, balancing on his toes and peering out between the bars.

A new dawn was rising on the town. Silhouetted against the white edge of the sun was a sharp-edged structure stretching up to the sky. Levi ran his gaze along the gallows, taking in the weather-worn planks of wood and frayed rope. He knew he should be scared for what was to come, but found he wasn't. In fact, he didn't feel much at all.

Levi also saw a creature perched on the far hillside. A fox. Its fur glinted in the reddish light, black eyes scanning the town. The animal paused, turned to the jailhouse, and seemed to look at the boy. Levi looked back. It shook its head and licked its jowls. Then, it scampered down the opposite side of the hill and out of sight.

The boy swallowed. He turned away, laid on the cot once again.

Levi would not live to witness many more dawns, he knew that for certain. But he took comfort in knowing there would never be one of them who wore his face.

Acknowledgements

This book was a labor of love. More than any of my other projects, the words flew onto the page effortlessly and once I started writing, it was impossible to stop. Although the subject matter is quite dark, it was a joy to work on and reinvigorated my passion for storytelling after several years of struggling with writer's block. That being said, *Ainsworth* never would've happened if it hadn't been for the following people:

To my loving parents: from Squigmire to Ainsworth, it's been quite the journey. Thank you for always supporting my work, no matter how macabre, and pushing me to do my best. I'm sorry for always making the parental figures dead, absent, or unhinged in my novels. One day, I promise I will write a book that includes parents as loving and caring as you both are.

In between *A Weighted Soul* and *Ainsworth*, I graduated college. While my degree may have nothing to do with writing, the friends I met there had everything to do with my survival during those four years. It was a pleasure working far into the night (and sometimes into the morning) on projects with you all and I truly hope you know how much you mean to me. You're all so talented and I can't wait to see what amazing careers and projects you take on next. Shoutouts to Jen, Corey, Bobby (and Lovie!), Genesis, Enzo, Marcello, Elizabeth, Matt, Uesli, Ron,

Mike, Eugene, Kayleigh, and Vanessa. Special shoutout to my senior design crew: long live DIBS!

Sardine Can crew, you guys are truly some of the best. I feel like you've watched me grow up quite literally and I'm so thrilled to get the chance to work alongside you. I promise to write the most unique and personalized messages in each of your copies of this book. Happy birthday, Manny!

High school friends who have stuck with me since the beginning, y'all are amazing. From my nervous excitement of publishing my debut to now, I'm forever grateful that you stuck by my side through it all. No matter how far apart we are, I'm always so grateful for when we finally catch up, even though it may be months or even years in between meet-ups. I wish the best for all of you.

How could I forget all the wonderful people who tune into my online content? Your support means the world to me and I cannot express how thankful I am that you take time out of your day to appreciate what I create. Thank you all!

I thank God for helping me utilize my gift in this creation and St. Francis de Sales for the prominent role he's played in my life. Veritas!

And to Chris. I'm so excited to finally dedicate one of my works to you, even if it's by far the least romantic I've ever written. Your unwavering belief and excitement in my dreams inspires me to be my best self each and every day. I can't wait to see what adventures the future has in store for us. I love you.

About the Author

J. L. Willow is the author of several works including the Amazon bestselling novel *Missing Her*. She graduated from Stevens Institute of Technology with a Bachelor of Engineering in mechanical engineering and a minor in engineering management. While she spends her days working in her field of study, her nights are spent dreaming up new thrilling (and often horrifying) tales.

About the Cover Designer & Illustrator

Crina Magalio is a published book illustrator, digital illustrator, and theatrical scenic designer. Her expressive illustrations are drawn by hand, inked, and colored digitally. She earned her Bachelor of Fine Arts degree in Illustration from the Maryland Institute College of Art in 2018.

Crina has worked with the Readington Community Theatre and created digitally drawn scenic designs for their 2018, 2019, and 2023 musical productions. She has worked with J. L. Willow, Lizbeth Ericka, and Dan Meyer. In her free time, she enjoys creating whimsical holiday themed illustrations every season! Crina hopes that J. L. Willow's readers enjoy this new mystery!